JANET OLEARSKI

was born in London and studied languages and linguistics at the University of Edinburgh, and the University of London Institute of Education. Her poetry and short fiction have appeared in *Wasafiri, Litro, Bare Fiction, Beautiful Scruffiness, The Commonline Journal* and elsewhere. She has authored several children's books, among them *Mr. Football, The Sunbird Mystery,* and *The Boy Who Never Smiled.* For adults she has published a short-story collection, *A Brief History of Several Boyfriends,* and a novel, *A Traveller's Guide to Namisa.* She is a graduate of the Manchester Writing School at Manchester Metropolitan University, and the founder of the Abu Dhabi Writers' Workshop. She has lived and worked in Italy, Poland, Oman, and the United Arab Emirates. She now lives in Central Portugal.

Read more at: www.janetolearski.com

Also By Janet Olearski

Adult Fiction

A Traveller's Guide to Namisa

Short Stories

A Brief History of Several Boyfriends

Books for Children

The Boy Who Never Smiled

Twins

Mr. Football

Three Fairy Tales

The Sunbird Mystery

As Editor and Contributor

The Write Stuff

THE BOOK OF REASONABLE WOMEN

Stories

Janet Olearski

Paperback: ISBN 978-989-53381-8-4
Ebook: ISBN 978-989-53381-9-1

Cover Design: ebooklaunch.com
Cover Image: The Metropolitan Museum of Art

For my mother Maureen Stark (1924-1991),
who taught me to be my own reasonable woman.

Contents

***

The Fire Narratives

Word got around that I was back. People didn't know about my lost job. Where the house was concerned, they guessed I would have called it a day and put the remains on the market. But no, I was starting anew, rising like the phoenix, flying towards a simpler life... in my carbonized ruin.

Perhaps some assumed I had money to burn, that I could buy and discard, as is the way with foreigners. All I had to burn was the house, and that had been done to perfection.

José had seen the house shortly after the fire. When he came in the door, he shook his head and asked in his language why I was still living there. I told him I had nowhere else to go. His eyes flickered, a sure sign that he didn't believe me for a minute.

It's not that I had invited him. He'd obviously come with an agenda. He blamed me, he said, for not insuring the house. I tried to explain that I thought it *had* been insured. In fact, the insurance had expired less than three months prior to the fire, roughly around the time I was lounging on a sunbed on the roof of my new house, refilling my glass with an icy beer brought from the fridge.

From his tone, you'd have thought the fire was my fault. The lack of a common language prevented me from explaining what had happened with the insurance, that I had entrusted the renewal to Carlos, and he had dragged his heels. But, yes, I did blame myself for not pursuing him and demanding he provide a fresh quote and a new policy. Did I really trust Carlos? I feel I did not. Secretly, perhaps I had never wanted him to take care of the insurance. I felt he was pulling a fast one, but I didn't know how he was pulling it. All this I wanted to explain to José, but I had not the words for it. I explained what I could, leaving the rest to José's imagination. He didn't in any case like Carlos. As José saw it, Carlos himself could have been blamed for winning my trust and taking my business away from him. I didn't like or trust either of them.

I made José a large cup of coffee with milk and sugar. I thought it best simply to make him something and let him not think that we expats were entirely lacking a sense of hospitality. The formulation of questions about preferences was beyond me.

José slipped off his jacket and placed it over the back of a chair. As he did so, I caught a whiff of stale aftershave. Essence of man. He set about inspecting the walls, tapping and shaking the exposed pipes. If he had done his job properly in the first place, the pipes might have been better protected from the heat and flames. Those pipes that were once copper-coloured were now blackened. Blackened also were the walls, the ceilings, the furniture. The imprints of my fingers and palms were stamped in soot all around the house. And who knew, said José, what would be found behind those walls? He could help me, but it would cost. I told him the municipality was going to take care of it, restoring all of the buildings devoured by the forest fires. I'm not sure if he grasped this, or if he *did* grasp it and did not want to believe it. People usually hoped, he said, that someone would save them, but the authorities always made promises they didn't keep. Seventy thousand Euros would be needed at the very least.

His coffee must now have been quite lukewarm. He took a gulp, then turned towards me and, looking directly into my eyes, I believe he said, 'Alicia, do you trust me?' I may have got that wrong.

The woman's name was Monica. She came the following afternoon, prompted by her boss, who had been prompted by my lawyer. She worked in social services, she told me. It was considered a good job, but it was a depressing one, this business of always dealing with people in trouble. For this reason, she worked in tandem with a counsellor. There was always a danger that someone despaired so much that they wanted to take their own life. She looked at me rather too directly when she said this. I wasn't yet ready to end it all but it was good to know that help was on hand. The counsellor hadn't been able to come that day since she was seeing her mother into an old people's home. The responsibility of having elderly family members had significantly impacted her work routines and her frame of mind.

I couldn't help thinking that this permanent state of associating with the misery of others showed on Monica's face, which was very rotund and bloated as if through the excessive consumption of comfort foods. Her lips were wide, fulsome, and plum-coloured, but they drooped at the corners, and no quantity of lip pencil could right them. Her hair, which was thick and dark and brushed back off her face, was laced with filigrees of silver. The skin under her eyes sagged very slightly in dark pockets and, throughout our conversation, her look hardly wavered with any change of expression. The days must have appeared alike for her even though each day must have been radically different from the one before.

She thumbed through the pages of my dossier. Evidently, I was well-documented. If I were to lose my memory, I could always revert to social services. Like me, she was alone, she said. She had noticed my status immediately when she reviewed my paperwork, and she hoped I didn't mind her bringing it up, since it was a topic, she felt, that had much relevance to my case and one that we two had in common.

In her case there had been opportunities, she said, but she had not taken them up. Her heart wasn't in them – in the opportunities. Her heart wasn't in those men. She was, or had been, 'taken.' She had given herself – heart and also soul – to a married man. She had given him the best years of her life. Wasn't that how they described it? At the outset, she thought he would leave his wife. At the time, she was not too bothered about whether they stayed together or not, but she became accustomed to him. This 'being accustomed,' she realised later, was love. And once she was hooked, she could not unhook herself so she continued as she was in this unsatisfactory arrangement.

Her friends, one in particular, berated her for wasting herself on this man. They knew him and hinted that she was not the first and probably not the last either. But, when all was said and done, the experience had made her a better person. At least she thought it had. She said she understood me completely wanting to live there alone in the house. Once you had had your chance, it was gone and it wasn't coming back, so it was best for the likes of us to resign ourselves to a life of exclusion and isolation. As she said this, she gazed with a saddened expression at the jacket hanging over the back of my chair.

I made her a cup of tea when in fact a glass of wine might have suited her better. She ticked a series of boxes on a printed document on her clipboard, and she thanked me for answering her questions.

In due course, social services would commence delivery of hot meals, which most likely would see me through the worst of the winter in my chilly, soot-encrusted home.

It was an acquaintance of an acquaintance who sent Armando. Unlike most people who knock at your front door or ring the bell, Armando rattled at the French windows at a time of day when I had drifted off to sleep on the sofa with a book in hand. He had come, he said, to cut the trees. He waved his hand in the direction of the charcoal stubs that protruded from the earth around the house. Because, he said, here there was 'a great danger for fire.' His argument was very persuasive. Having endured one fire, I did not want to be the victim of a second. As he spoke, he placed his hand on my arm so he could be sure that, in the absence of comprehension, his message was all the more pointed. Judging by the breath he puffed into my face, a few early beers had passed his way. I invited him to step inside and drink another, which he was very happy to do. He had not seen the inside of the house before and had plenty to say, most of which I did not understand. You could smell the fire, he said, even after six months or more had passed. I did not really have the language to tell him that the odour of burnt house came from the no-good wood burner that José had installed for me the summer before – further evidence to my mind that people believe what they want to believe or what they feel they *should* believe. Tell them there's been a flood and they'll say they can smell the flood waters, when in fact it's only water dribbling out of the back of the washing machine.

It wasn't easy, he said, to live in the country when all you know is the city. Many people came here, but they lasted hardly any time at all. He'd been caught out by this himself. He'd met a very attractive woman on a trip to Lisbon one year. He'd met her in the *padaria,* buying bread. They'd struck up a conversation. She was a woman of some class, an intellectual. Who would have thought she'd find an interest in him? He thought it would fizzle out then and there, but she seemed impressed with his stories of life in the country, possibly even envious of them. She was a university lecturer, a free thinker, a lover of traditional ways. More than anything she wanted to make that all-important shift back to nature, back to a life among trees, vegetation, wildlife. The pastoral life.

He found her a rental cottage for the summer, one that a friend of his had renovated. It had stood empty for some time since there were few adventurous souls like her who sought the campestral life. It was out of the way, which she said she did not mind at all since she needed peace and quiet to work on her research. Why… she might even write a novel, she told him, and for that she could not be dealing with the noisy interruptions that you encountered all the time in the city. The location, up at the top of an unmade lane, did not trouble her in the slightest. The landscape, she felt, was inspiring, apart from the container yard to the right that, with its ragged silhouette, obstructed her view of the forest.

The cottage had a sizeable garden that was significantly overgrown and unmanicured. Armando felt it apt that he could apply his skills to ameliorate the life of the woman who was now so close to his heart. As he pruned her trees and trimmed her plants, she would be snipping away and removing the unwanted baggage of her complex life. That the cottage was set in a place of great seclusion suited them both as it was safe from the prying eyes of the villagers. The through road did, of course, pass in front of the village's only café, and he found it annoying to see watches checked and even glasses raised as he drove by.

The woman, meanwhile, was thinking long term. She might extend the rental or even buy, both options which suited Armando's friend very well. Armando himself advised her that she needed to see if she could sit it out for a couple of winters before she considered buying, and she should perhaps look at other areas. The truth was he was slightly miffed that she might pay his friend's inflated tariff. He knew the fellow had got the place dirt cheap and had paid a pittance to some Senegalese laborers to do the work, and now Armando, through this introduction, was putting wads of Euros into his friend's open palm. In addition, the garden was being landscaped for free. Out of love, or infatuation. Armando was not as yet sure into which category his emotions fell.

Almost from the outset he gathered that her vision of country living might be grossly off the mark. There was talk of beekeeping, the ownership of sheep, and the gathering of fresh eggs every morning from free-range chickens. He promised her they would talk of bees after the summer, but he could not dissuade her from the chickens and the sheep. To his annoyance, his friend provided the sheep. Special ones and, for that, especially expensive.

It was true that they kept down the grass, but removing the corpse of the one that died from misfeeding caused too much of a song and dance for his liking, and he was unaccustomed to dealing with the degree of hysteria it generated. The woman told him that she might well have bonded with the sheep if it hadn't been for the torrential rain that continued through the early summer months. The sheep were sold on to the café owner, who said he would serve up at least one of them during festivities for the patron saint's day the following month. When the woman heard this, she decided she had indeed bonded with the sheep but, by then, it was too late. Of the chickens, one was fatally savaged by a fox, and the other expired, possibly of old age, on the floor of the woodshed. After that, the woman relied on Armando to fetch her fresh eggs, though she ceased to cook any after reading a particularly convincing article about cholesterol.

I directed Armando to the bathroom after he finished his second beer, and I apologized to him for the grime and oily soot that adhered to the walls, the floor and the porcelain accessories. He was gone some time and I eventually found him outside, standing ankle deep in rubble as he finished a cigarette. I was impressed that he was gracious enough not to smoke in the house. I brought him a third bottle of *Sagres*. He took a last draw on his cigarette and threw it into the garden. It was like this, he told me, now obviously in contemplative mood, this woman was not cut out for country pursuits. You cannot keep your mind filled with enriching thoughts for the entire length of every single day, he said. However much the woman thought she could keep herself both amused and productive, she was deluding herself. He could only be there with her for a few hours a day, and even in that short space of time, they were running out of things to say.

He found her diminished. In truth, she was diminished before. He just hadn't noticed. He liked a woman with some flesh on her, he said. She could never have stood the chill blasts of winter winds with that thin translucent skin of hers, those hollowed-out cheeks, the long artistic fingers, the nails of which would have turned blue in the frozen air. She needed diversions. She needed connections. Which is why, when arriving at the cottage in an unscheduled slot of free time, he found his friend's pickup parked outside.

Presumably, this was the very same pickup that was now being parked in my driveway, its owner coming to retrieve the jacket he had left behind. Armando stopped himself in mid-sentence. José had hardly set foot inside the doorway when a third vehicle drew up, a minivan with the municipality's red and green crest imprinted on its side. The scene that followed after Monica had stepped over the threshold was worthy of a Brazilian soap opera.

Armando's eyes, previously somnolent from an excess of afternoon beers – *mea culpa* – now opened wide. He looked first at me and then back at José. José, for his part, stared initially at Armando and then at me. I smiled. A feeble attempt at damage limitation. Monica, meanwhile, stood paralyzed on the threshold, holding my packed lunch close to her chest. She looked firstly at José, then at me, then away again, to study the blotched and fire-stained floor tiles at her feet.

'Here,' I told her, prising the package from her hands, 'let me take that.'

I left them there, and slipped into the kitchen to have my lunch. No point in letting it get cold. I heard raised voices. I do believe they had forgotten about me. I poured myself a glass of *Altano*, and carried it outside with my meal to the once-porch where the brittled tiles crunched underfoot. I made myself comfortable on a melted garden chair. Far in the distance, across a landscape of charred roof beams and roasted fruit trees, I could see a lake of mist sinking onto the tall skeletons of the eucalyptus forest. Some broken things, I reflected - a house, for example - you can repair. Other things may not be worth the bother. How easily one can become collateral damage. In life, I realised, it was always best to avoid falling into someone else's narrative. You have enough on your hands with your own.

Drinking my wine, I let time relax, and hoped only that José would remember to take his jacket with him when he left.

***

The Empty Suit

She supposed that, while she was sleeping, her mother must have entered her room, because when she got up, she found that a man's suit had been laid out on top of the bookcase next to the window. She had the sense that her mother might possibly have taken something from the wardrobe, but it couldn't have been the suit. The suit, she didn't recognize. On reflection, she realised it was more like a child's suit than a man's, the kind of outfit a ventriloquist's dummy might wear, with a little white collar, a tie, a flower in the lapel, and a handkerchief in its top pocket. The suit was like a small body lying there, though there was no person or no body inside it. It was as though it had just come from the cleaners. Maybe her mother had thought to put it in the wardrobe, but had then decided it would be better to lay it down, to spread it out.

After she had thought of all these things and remained puzzled, she got back into bed. She was fully dressed and had gone to bed because weariness and cold had overcome her. Under the covers, she curled into a warm ball and fell asleep again.

Later, when she awoke and the room was as it had been when she first entered, she wondered why her mother, dead all these years, would have brought her that empty little suit.

***

Storm Cakes

They said there was a storm brewing. Claire couldn't see it herself. She looked out of her window and searched for storm clouds, but there were none. This was the Arabian Gulf after all. What was the worst they could expect? A sandstorm? Half an hour of light rain? The sky was white and silent, just as it had been for the past few days. Other than that, there was nothing especially untoward about the weather. As far as she could tell, the only thing that would be brewing was the cup of tea she was about to make herself in the office kitchen.

On her way down the corridor, she passed colleagues hastening to their cars, carrying with them the briefcases and bags they had brought with them earlier that day. A minor exodus was in progress. It was barely halfway through the morning and nowhere near midday, but as she stirred her tea it occurred to her that what she needed now was a cake – or maybe two – to tide her over until lunchtime. She was thinking along the lines of a chunky chocolate cake with a praline filling, perhaps something between a biscuit and a cake so that when you sank your teeth into it, the chocolate resisted and then crumbled into rich cocoa pieces that merged into a soft crème. Or, she might settle for a sweet pastry, filled with a finely textured almond paste and topped with icing, so that when you bit into it, your teeth left a deep indentation. Better still, she could imagine a block of vanilla cream, sandwiched between a double-layered slice of fudge-covered puff pastry. She sighed with cake-driven desire.

Back at her desk, she found an email sent 'with high importance.' The storm was on its way, it said, according to the latest warning from the Meteorological Office. She was instructed to pack up immediately and go home. For the second time that morning, she scrutinized the sky. Yes, it was a little grey. Yes, it was a little windy, but to call it a storm was the stuff of wimps. Back home in Nottingham, she would think nothing of trudging through snow to meet a friend, or of pressing through driving rain to get her shopping. And here all they were expecting was a high wind and it was the end of the world.

The road she took was not the most direct to her home in Khalifa City. She had identified her priorities, and her priorities were cakes. So, she drove through the swirling dust clouds, past the waving fronds of the date palms and pulled up outside her favourite coffee shop. Inside, she began to browse the cakes. Wasn't she already over her regular weight? Yes, she was, but disrupted from her routine by the storm that never was, she sought and deserved compensation. In short, she didn't *need* cakes but she *wanted* them, and would have them. And, they looked too delicious to walk away from.

As she considered all of this, a woman bustled into the café accompanied by a young girl of about eight or nine, possibly her granddaughter. Together they also examined the cakes.

Behind the counter, the assistant prepared a cake box. Was Claire ready to choose, she asked. Claire wasn't. There was much to take into consideration when choosing cakes. It was first necessary to imagine flavours and textures.

And, as Claire did this, the woman started to make her choice: 'One of these, one of those, two of the chocolate ones, maybe one carrot cake with the icing. The pink one. No, the green one. The one with the strawberries and kiwi on top.' She conferred with the little girl. 'Do you want one of those, or one of these?'

As she chose, the assistant removed the cakes from the display. Claire's gaze would alight on a cake and it would be removed then and there before her. 'And a custard slice,' said the woman. And Claire thought, 'Oh, I wanted that!' And then the woman would indicate a chocolate cheesecake slice, and that too would be removed. '*Well, that's gone then,*' thought Claire. Still, cakes remained.

'Is that eight?' said the woman.

'Yes,' said the assistant. 'Now you can take another eight for free.'

'*What?*' thought Claire. '*There's an offer on? I could take eight, and eight for free, but then I'd have had to eat them all myself.*' Not that she couldn't do it ... just that she shouldn't do it ... mustn't do it.

And as she thought these thoughts, more cakes disappeared from the display as the eight free cakes were added to the cake box. The chocolate mousse – gone. The fudge slice – gone. The pistachio cake – gone. Now Claire felt like saying, 'Give a girl a break. Leave something for me.'

In all of this, the woman never once cast a glance in Claire's direction, never acknowledged her presence. There was no cake camaraderie from her side. Claire stood there, invisible, watching the disappearance of the cakes.

When they were safely in the box, a second assistant asked Claire what she would like. Claire felt inclined to say, 'Well there's not much left to choose from, is there?' But she kept her mouth shut and made her choice, swiftly this time, otherwise all would be lost. She took just two cakes that would rattle about in an otherwise empty box.

By now the woman had handed over her card to make her payment. The assistant swiped once, then a second time, then a third.

'The card isn't working,' she said.

'I've just used it in the supermarket,' said the woman.

'No, look,' said the assistant, 'it isn't going through.' She swiped again.

The little girl stared at Claire as she collected her cake box and handed over her money. Claire smiled at her, but the girl gave a twisted half smile and turned away. There it was, thought Claire. She had been rejected by both generations: granddaughter and grandmother. The discussion about the card continued, until a second woman, not unlike the first – mother to the little girl and daughter to the cake woman – entered the café and joined the conversation.

'What's the problem?' she said.

'The card's not working, madam,' said the assistant.

'How is it not working? We've just used it in the supermarket.'

And this is where Claire wanted to help, remembering that sometimes if you give a credit card a quick clean or a polish, it starts working again. Maybe there was grunge on the card or maybe there was dust in the card swipe machine. It had happened to her before. She was about to step forward and make the suggestion when she hesitated. She had forgotten how she didn't exist for them, how she wasn't anybody. Was she now going to chip in with a helpful suggestion? Her inner voice said, '*No, actually. Let them sort it out for themselves.*'

As she headed for the door, one of the women said again, 'How can the card not work. We've only just used it in the supermarket.' And Claire thought that two cakes in the box were better than sixteen on the counter.

A spray of rain hit her as she reached her car, but all was well now that she had her cakes. '*Let the storm come*,' she thought.

And it did.

As she drove, a black cloud descended on her from a metal sky. The traffic lights swung maniacally above her head, shovel loads of sand slopped across her windscreen. The day turned to night, the clouds opened, and torrential rain fell hammering onto her car. She drove on, the wind buffeting her back and forth across the four-lane highway, the cake box wobbling and bouncing on her passenger seat. Jagged knives of light shot down from the sky. She couldn't stop, nor could she pull over. She couldn't even see the edges of the road. All she saw were occasional pinpoints of light – the tail lights of the cars in front.

When she reached the roundabout, which she did not know she had reached, she crashed into it, and then drove over it and continued on to take her exit. But, because she could see nothing in that grey fuzz of sand and rain and wind, she overshot her exit and crashed into the pavement. So, she drove over the pavement and did a second full circuit of the roundabout until, following the glinting car lights, she found her way out and drove forward to the next roundabout, trying to stay straight in her lane though she had lost all sense of orientation. All the while, she beat down her panic, her terror, telling herself she must now be close to home and, once home, she would be safe. And there would be cake.

But when she negotiated the next roundabout in the driving rain, blind in that cloak of daytime night, and aimed for the exit to her street, she missed, overshot and crashed onto the side reservation. She tried now to reverse back down, but her gears were jammed and her tyres spinning. She switched off the engine, switched back on, went into first, drove forward onto the road, drove with flattened tyres, on steel, to another exit.

But where was she? She ploughed through lakes of water, winding down the window and leaning out into the downpour to fathom where she was and, seeing a street that looked vaguely familiar, she found she was driving away from home, not towards it. She reversed, inhaling the smell of burning in her car. She drove forward across another mini-roundabout, the rain relenting slightly now. And there, rattling along the road, she found her driveway.

Her car tyres flapped, the rubber smoked and burned. The hubcaps were crushed, the bumper cracked and coloured yellow and black from the paintwork that she had brought back with her from the roundabouts, the gear box wrecked. '*Woe is me,*' she thought as the sky cleared and she stood before her wreck of a vehicle.

And then, as Claire retrieved her cake box from the passenger seat, a disturbing thought came to her. She had made a dreadful mistake, a catastrophic error. Whatever could have provoked her to buy only two cakes?

***

Nairobi

Nairobi, at the Norfolk Hotel, the first morning after her arrival, Amanda orders room service. The waiter comes with her breakfast. In movies, people in pyjamas or negligees think nothing of opening hotel doors to strangers, but Amanda is not like them. She greets her waiter fully dressed.

Bearing her tray is a shiny-faced man in green and khaki livery. The name Joseph is engraved on the brass-plated badge he wears on his lapel. Joseph asks if she has slept well and follows with a barrage of other questions. How does she like Kenya? How was her journey? How far has she travelled?

When she tells him that she is from London, that this is her first visit, that she is sure she is going to like Kenya very much, he seems to her to be unusually overwhelmed.

"London! You are from London!" he says. "I welcome you, Miss Amanda, to my beautiful country." And with that, he opens his arms, pulls her to him, grasps her in a bear hug, and kisses her on both cheeks.

It all happens so suddenly and so unexpectedly that she hasn't even time to flinch. She stands there confounded. Amanda is a woman alone in a hotel room in the arms of a complete stranger, who has just kissed her.

'Oh,' she says, 'thank you.' She signs her bill and holds the door open as he leaves smiling and fingering a generous tip.

And Amanda thinks, *I suppose that must be their way here in Nairobi.*

***

With My Little Eye

It was a stupid thing that happened. Mia had gone round the back of the house to do a good deed that no one had asked her to do, to feed a stray cat. The animal was a mangy character, covered in deep red-ripped scratches like someone had attacked him with a garden rake. She leaned over him and emptied out onto the ground some left over mince scraped from the dinner plates – rather this than let it go to waste. The cat slavered, tossed back its head and a globule of saliva flew into her eye. She recoiled, blinked and trapped the slime inside her eyelid. That's how it started, or how she supposed it must have started because sometimes in life we just need an explanation, however implausible.

In the days that followed, it was as if her mind were in two places at once. Behind her, as she stood washing the dishes and looking out of the kitchen window, her son Peter. In front of her, in the next garden, her new neighbour. Difficult to choose the focus of one's attention. For a mother, it should be the child. For the wife, it may well be the newcomer. As it was, the two images overlapped and her head spun.

'I spy with my little eye something beginning with… "B"'

Peter's mouth was lightly edged with biscuit crumbs. He said, 'You've got your back turned, Mum.'

'I can see you,' said Mia, 'and you need to stop it.'

Roy looked up from his newspaper. 'Mums can see everything,' he said.

Mia looked over her shoulder, suspending her work at the sink. 'Yes, everything.' And, as she spoke, she glimpsed down at her shoulder and noticed two long dark hairs lying on the pile of her cardigan. She puffed at them and they floated to the kitchen floor. 'Have to get my hair trimmed sometime soon,' she said.

That afternoon, as she brushed her hair, she noted a batch of strands in her hairbrush. Maybe it wasn't a haircut she needed, but a change of shampoo, or perhaps a change of diet. She hoped not. She picked up her hand mirror and, juggling reflections, strained to see the back of her head. From the garden outside, she could hear voices. She put down the mirror for a moment and moved to the window. Roy was leaning up against the fence, chatting to a young blonde woman. What was her name? Sofie, Stella, Simone? Something like that. Mia felt a pang of irritation. Or was it jealousy? She should have had no gripes about this woman. She was nice enough, but this was *her* territory and that was *her* husband. She squinted in the late afternoon sun. She couldn't quite see their expressions from this distance. She covered her right eye. Her vision was indistinct. She covered her left eye and the picture came clear again. Surely it wasn't time for glasses? Not at her age, not so young.

She took up the mirror again and scrutinized that eye. It looked glassy, as though an infection was about to take hold. She pressed the skin above her cheekbone, pulling down the lower lid. The membrane was unusually pink, and tiny ragged lines of red capillaries spread across the base of her eyeball like miniscule creepers. A thin film of mucus floated into the corner of her eye, but the blur remained. From outside, a peal of laughter reached her. She sighed. Here she was, battling with approaching middle age and all was well with the new neighbour. Too well perhaps.

It didn't especially surprise her that within twenty-four hours, an infection had taken hold in her left eye. She stared at the raw redness of it. The tissue had swollen around the eyeball and threatened to close the whole eye. It rendered her pupil and iris small and pinched as though, in fearfulness, they were falling backwards into an abyss of brain and gore. Mia saw only muggily through the swelling. That morning, when Peter was safely delivered onto the school bus and Roy at work, she took time to investigate the source and extent of the irritation. How could it have come to this? What was it? Hairs from the cat? Tainted mascara? Dust? Whatever had caused it made her look like a prizefighter, as though someone had poked a malicious finger into malleable tissue. Gently, she prised open the eyelid. Her left eye seemed almost to be veering inwards towards her nose. In fact, that was what she saw... her nose. On the side of her nose was a large inflamed spot. That was what she could see. With her eye in that position, the white of it straining out of place, the iris pulling inwards, she felt nauseous, woozy. She stepped falteringly towards the bathroom and threw up.

After examining her, the doctor took a look at her falling hair, scrutinising her scalp.

'It's very thin,' she told him. 'You know... at the back. The front seems okay.'

'Hmm...' he said. He looked perplexed. At least that's how it seemed to her. 'Well, for the eye, I can give you some ointment,' he said. 'It'll soon clear up, but you'll need to make sure you don't go strolling about if it's windy outside. You could keep the eye covered up, or just wear sunglasses.'

'Not if it's raining,' she said.

'Well, you know what I mean,' he said. 'For the hair, you can take silica. You can get some from the chemist's.' He paused and squinted at her. 'It could be stress-related. From what you've told me, you seem to be eating well enough, so I doubt it's your diet. Are you under any stress at the moment?'

She thought she was, but she was darned if she was going to tell him. This business with Roy, his shifty and irregular behavior. He could have been behaving that way because of her. She'd been less than accommodating since the eye problem and – let's face it – she was beginning to look like someone out of a horror movie. The way she looked with her eye closed and the left side of her face swollen, her hair like rats' tails. Surely that would turn anyone off?

'Mum,' said Peter when she got back and started to make his tea. 'You know what?'

'No, what?'

'I can see your skull.'

'Don't be weird,' she said. But he wasn't being weird. She was the weird one.

When he was in front of the TV and eating his supper, she locked herself in the downstairs bathroom and, applying a sleight of mirrors, she saw her bony white pate shining out from under a few meagre strands of dark hair. But this could not be her. She rearranged her head. She covered the gaps and fixed her hairwork with spray.

It was round about the same time she started to see bright kaleidoscopic lights that she felt the swelling on the back of her head. She ran her fingers over it several times, testing for pain. It was sore and it seemed huge, but she reflected that this was often the case with spots and infections. They seemed massive to the touch, but in reality, they were just pimple-sized when you saw them in the mirror. She smoothed her fingers over the bump, and they came away sticky as though she had disturbed a suppurating wound. As she guided herself up the stairs, clinging to the bannister, she felt off kilter, unbalanced. What she told herself was that her body would right itself. It was just a question of time.

'Why didn't you ask the doctor to send you to a specialist?' said Roy.

'Oh, *I* get it! This is *my* fault, is it?'

'I'm just saying,' said Roy.

'Yes, well, I'm saying that when I went to see him, it wasn't like this. It's just got worse over the last few days.'

Waking up that morning, Mia's eye did not open. It was as if it were glued shut.

'Are you sure you're using the ointment?' said Roy.

'Of course I am,' she snapped. 'It's probably the ointment that's sealing it.'

In the bathroom, she washed her face with soapy water, bathing carefully around her left eye. It occurred to her that the swelling had subsided slightly. If anything, she had the sensation that the area around the eye had flattened as though sunken into its socket. That couldn't be bad, could it?

By the time she reached the kitchen, Roy had gone, skipping his breakfast and leaving even before the arrival of the morning newspaper. So, she thought, you can't stomach seeing me like this over your boiled egg. She could not say why but she derived some satisfaction from this. She went in search of her sunglasses.

'They look stupid, Mum,' said Peter when he saw her. 'People will laugh.'

'Shut your mouth,' said Mia.

Peter stared at her for a moment, then looked away. He did as she said. He shut his mouth. Without another word, Mia saw him to the school gate. With the school bus out of service, and Roy long gone, delivering him had fallen to her this overcast morning. On her way back to the car, she was buffeted by an icy gale. She cursed the wind for unmaking her hair. Then she cursed her child and she cursed her child's useless cheating father. She cursed them both for undoing her.

As she leaned down to open the car door, she saw one of the mothers making her way towards her. It didn't occur to her *how* she saw her, but she did. The woman was right behind her before she knew it.

'Mia?' said the woman. 'Are you all right?'

Before turning to face her, as if in a haze, Mia saw an expression of alarm on the woman's face.

'Peter told James you'd hurt your eye. Is it better now?'

Mia turned and removed her sunglasses. 'No,' she said, 'it's not.'

The woman froze, stepped back, gasped.

'What's the matter?' said Mia. 'Never seen an eye infection?'

The woman hesitated, swallowed.

'Yes?' said Mia.

'Is there anything I can do?' said the woman.

'Such as…?' said Mia.

The woman gaped at Mia's fibrous hair, flapping in the wind.

'Mmm?' said Mia. 'Spit it out.'

'Your hair,' said the woman. She took a breath, then spoke again. 'I could give you an address. A trichologist. To help you with your hair, I mean.'

'Piss off,' said Mia, and she got into the car and started up the engine. As she drove away, she saw two images merged – the road ahead and the woman shocked and bemused staring after her.

Roy told her he was going on a business trip. Who was he kidding? She could see right through him.

'Go,' she said as she packed food into the fridge. 'You won't be missed.' She could see the dismay on his face without even looking.

'I don't know what's up with you,' he said. 'I can't seem to do anything right these days.'

'But you're getting on all right with your girlfriend.'

'What?' he said.

'I'm watching you,' she said. 'I know what you're up to.'

That morning when she picked up Roy's discarded clothes, she had smelled perfume, not *her* perfume, and not aftershave. From the window at the front of the house, she watched him walk to his car. But she saw him only with her good eye.

Returning to her room, she pushed aside her hair and looked at herself in the mirror. The flesh around her other eye had grown thick and smooth across her face. All that remained of what had once been her eye was a row of tufts: her eyelashes, now buried, like grass sprouting through earth. It seemed almost normal to her. Was she to remove the tips of those buried lashes with depilatory cream? She thought better of it. She smoothed her fingers over the tufts and the dip of smooth skin, and began to hum a little tune.

With Roy away, it was just her and Peter. Mia poured herself a glass of wine. Hers was a sense of liberation and power. No burdens. No obstructions. It seemed there was much that no longer mattered to her. Her hair, growing thicker, draped her face like a ponderous shroud, leaving free her strong eye, powerful, all-seeing, miraculous. She reveled in the thought that nature was taking its course, allowing her to become what she so needed to become. She had never been her true self. Until now, she had not seen clearly.

At the window, wine glass in hand, she followed the movements of her neighbour, while noting with satisfaction that she could see images from the television, viewed by her now silent child on the opposite side of the room. At first, the images had been indistinct, but – as the days passed – they grew sharper.

In the shower, she fingered the swollen lump that had remained on the back of her head. Some kind of abscess? She needed to sort that out. The doctor needed to sort it out. He was the one who had said her eye would clear up when it hadn't.

'It sounds like an abscess,' said the doctor. 'No worries. We can lance it, and then put you on antibiotics for a week or so.'

'All right,' she said. 'You seem to think you know best.' But even as she said that, she knew that really only she knew best.

He parted the hair on the back of her head, and she watched with infinite calm as he stopped and drew back in horror. He returned to his desk. He coughed. He drank some water.

'I'll give you a referral letter for the hospital,' he said, all the while looking down and not at her. 'Just ring them up and ask for an appointment.'

In the surgery, still sitting on the examination couch with her back turned to him, she studied with a certain fascination the implements he was to have used on the abscess. These were, she thought, sharp, rather dangerous tools best kept out of the reach of a child or someone who might be slightly unstable. As she made these observations, she watched him and listened to the scratching of his pen. She saw how with trembling hands he folded the letter and placed it inside an envelope.

'I've written the phone number and the extension on the envelope,' he said.

She stood up and crossed the room to his desk. Looking away, he held out the letter. 'Forget it,' she said. 'You're just wasting my time.'

He looked up, and into the one eye that stared first at him and then at the object she held in her hand.

'That's a surgical instrument,' he said. 'You are not a doctor. You need to put that back right now.'

Driving back, Mia saw the familiar figure of her neighbour walking along the lane towards home. The woman smiled and gave her a wave as she drove past. The bag she carried looked too heavy for one of such a lightweight, delicate appearance. Mia stopped the car some distance ahead and waited as the woman, quickening her pace, came towards her. Mia slipped the vehicle into reverse and put her foot on the accelerator. She found that driving was so much simpler now that she could dispense with the use of mirrors.

Mia embraced her child then, cupping his chin in one hand, she wiped the tear from his eye. 'Nothing to worry about,' she said.

'Will I have to go to the hospital?' he said.

'Of course not. It'll be fine. You'll see.' And she stroked his hair, smoothing her fingers over the small protuberance on the back of his head. 'Everything comes right by itself,' she said. 'You'll understand so much more when that happens. You'll see them coming… all those boys who've ever teased you. Boys like James. You don't like him, do you?'

'No,' said Peter.

'No,' said Mia. 'And his mother isn't nice either. That's how James got to be so nasty. His mother taught him. There are so many horrible people in this world, Peter, but you've got the edge on them. You'll always know what they're going to do before they do it. No one will ever take you by surprise. Never. Ever.'

Mia removed her sunglasses and looked at herself in the mirror. Where her inflamed left eye had been, her skin was smooth and clear. She scooped some moisturizer from a tiny tub on her dressing table and massaged it across her cheeks and under her eye. She liked the way her face had become more symmetrical, her gaze centred and balanced as it stared out from beneath her lush curtain of ebony hair. Reflected in the full-length mirror by the bedroom door, she could see the back of her head. She saw this image even more clearly once she had parted her hair and pushed it away from the nape of her neck.

She heard the sound of a key in the lock, and then Roy's voice.

'Mia?'

'Upstairs,' she called back. And she listened for the tread of his footsteps. The faintest trace of scent preceded him. It might well have been aftershave but – more likely – perfume. Mia sat at her dressing table relishing the world of insight bequeathed her by that all-seeing eye.

And, when Roy entered the room, from behind her veil of inky strands, it gave her immense pleasure to see, with her little eye, the terror on his face.

***

Priorities

Even though you will rarely find her sitting at her desk, for added comfort there is a gold-edged cushion propped against the back of her empty chair. At right angles to her workspace, there is a low grey filing cabinet – unused – on which there stands a framed photograph of one of the many grandsons of the much-loved Sheikh. It is an image of a child now grown to adulthood and inherited importance.

In the littered in-trays lie receipts for her own children's school fees paid for by her employer. On the backs of envelopes and photocopied medical certificates are scribbled to-do lists in Arabic and in English, for the maids, the gardener and the driver, and drawings of multilayered wedding gowns that she has doodled while talking on her iPhone. Her bling-covered Blackberry lies abandoned by a catalogue of the last *Bride Show* in Dubai.

Next to her office phone is a box of embossed *Wedding World* business cards. A small glass teacup containing wilted mint leaves sits unwashed in its matching saucer on top of a company notification of the declared holiday and a greetings card with the words 'Eid Mubarak' printed in ornate script on the outside. In the waste bin is a sheet of tightly crumpled paper bearing the company logo, with the printed words 'Warning Letter' just discernible along its upper margin.

***

Holiday

It was unfortunate that on the first day of Miss Winter's holiday, a small brown bug fell out of the spongy folds of her bread roll. She suppressed her horror, resolving not to make a public exhibition of her plight or, through her alarm, to incite a minor exodus from the hotel dining room. It was always wiser not to fuss.

The waiter stood at her side. 'Coffee, madam?'

'Thank you,' replied Miss Winter. She withheld this secret knowledge of the bug. It had, after all, been her decision, her resolution, to open her mind, to accept, and to experience. But she still had the nagging doubt that she was not ready for all this. Indeed, that she might never be ready for it. There were the years she had spent reading of these places, imagining them, seeing herself exploring them. As always, the reality was quite different.

She looked down at her plate. This nasty little insect was part and parcel of the new life she had promised herself. She was travelling to broaden her mind and the bug was there to help her broaden it. She felt a degree of guilt at having been the recipient of this unpleasant creature. She scrutinised it, straining through her glasses and pushing it, repulsed, to the furthest corner of her plate with the tip of her knife.

'There is something wrong, madam?'

She started at the intrusion of this unexpected voice and slid her glasses rapidly from her nose. She smiled at the waiter.

'Thank you,' she said. 'Everything's fine.' But she wondered if it would stay fine and how soon it would be before the appearance of her next creepy-crawly. She might take sliced bread tomorrow.

Sipping her coffee, she considered her holiday. She had achieved much. She had made a booking. She had endured her first flight. She was in her first foreign country. She was alone. She considered herself very courageous. Her feat, in its own small way, was equal to the feats of those first women travellers. A step forward for womankind. She had much to praise herself for. She dreamed on, her eyes transfixed, staring through the open window of the breakfast room onto the green leafy courtyard below, where two of the cleaning girls in pale blue smocks stood laughing and chatting in their rapid, incomprehensible language. The waiters wove speedily in and out of tables, conferring at intervals about tablecloths that needed to be changed, knives and forks that were to be replaced – and bread rolls, possibly containing foreign bodies, that were to be delivered to others who would certainly denounce them.

The day boded well. It promised sunshine and warmth. She was not ready yet to venture outside the walls of the hotel. She must first have a measure of the place. She took photographs of the pool from various angles. The attendant brought her a sun bed and set her in a row with other morning bathers.

'You are from England?' he said.

'Yes,' she replied. She was not sure if it was advisable to converse.

'It is your first visit?' he continued.

'Yes,' she said. Her first ever, anywhere, she thought.

He was a heavily built man, much younger than her.

'You are alone?' he said.

She was alone.

'You tell me when you want – I shall take you visit town,' he said.

She did not wish to offend. 'I prefer to be alone,' she said.

'I shall take you to nightclub,' he said. 'You shall enjoy very much.'

No, she did not think she would enjoy very much.

'I come back later,' said the pool attendant. His friend was calling him.

She hoped he would not come back later. Her eyes closed. She lay in the sun inventing her excuses.

'There are ants in my room,' Miss Winter spoke slowly and clearly.

The receptionist listened to her words, but remained expressionless. Miss Winter thought she might not have understood.

'There are ants in my room,' she repeated. 'On the floor by my bed. Ants.' She did not know how else she might convey this phenomenon.

The receptionist shifted uneasily. 'You have fear to sleep?' she queried, and waited motionless for a response.

Miss Winter imagined the insidious advance of these creatures up the towering heights of her bedpost and across the white deserts of her pillow. Yes, Miss Winter did have fear to sleep. But it was not so much a question of ants, rather a greater issue. A cultural matter perhaps. She doubted herself. It called into question her ability to adapt.

'You want I send someone?' said the receptionist. This showed a degree of intuition on her part.

'Yes,' said Miss Winter, yielding. 'Yes, please,' she said.

'I send,' said the receptionist.

The receptionist did not send. Miss Winter feared the critical eye of the spray carrier. Late into the night she sat fully dressed on the edge of her bed, her slippered feet supported on a chair. She charted the progress of the enemy troops on the ground. She did not change for bed until the early hours.

The morning sun dusted lightly across Miss Winter's undefined body. She lay listening to the splashes and the children's voices, her book still unread by her side. A shadow fell over her.

'You have see the beach?' said the pool attendant.

No, Miss Winter had not yet seen the beach. She had attempted the promenade with its cafes and souvenir shops. There were many curious eyes. She had retreated in haste.

'I take you,' he confirmed.

Miss Winter was busy. The man was suspicious. It did not appear to him that Miss Winter was busy.

'It is difficult,' he said sagely. 'Woman alone.' He continued. 'They ask, you say, I am married woman. I have American husband. This answer is good,' he said.

At the postcard stand, she was well in control. She did not want kaftans or brass pots or ceramic plates.

'Yes, you want,' they told her.

No, she did not want, she told them.

'You are alone,' said the shop owner. 'I think you want I take you tonight to dance.'

Miss Winter scrutinised the man through her sunglasses. 'I am a married woman,' she told him. 'I have an American husband.'

'Ah,' said the shopkeeper, and he spoke quickly and obscurely to his companion. They both looked at her again, but said no more. She bought her cards and left. This answer is good, thought Miss Winter, and she hastened home to her hotel, radiant with achievement.

Miss Winter was busy on Saturday night. Very busy. The pool attendant was perplexed. He saw no evidence of her busy-ness.

'I wait you come,' he told the unwilling Miss Winter.

'No,' said Miss Winter. She had an appointment with friends.

'I wait,' said the man. 'You will come.'

Miss Winter was finding her holiday stressful. In her room, she flicked from channel to channel, watching five minutes here and ten minutes there. She explored the mini bar. She read – of women travellers – and she observed the progress of the ants by her bed. They had accepted her now. She had almost accepted them.

'I wait. Why you no come?' announced the pool attendant moodily when she emerged as usual after breakfast.

Miss Winter had been with her friends. The man shook his head mournfully and disappeared to the opposite side of the pool. Her lounger was not in its usual place. It was not there at all.

Her holiday was not as she had expected. She stood on her balcony now, her bathing things still tucked under her arm. Couples walked past along the promenade below. Groups of men strolled in conversation, their arms linked. In the distance, she could see the sea. She could not reach it. She was alone. She had an American husband. She sat in a white plastic chair and looked at the still blue sky. She could see little else from here except for the dusty terrace tiles and the open windows of other hotel rooms.

'Today, no swim?' asked the blue-smocked cleaning lady. She was concerned for Miss Winter.

'I like it here,' said Miss Winter. 'Here is good.'

The woman disappeared. Miss Winter closed her eyes and felt the sun's warmth and, in her mind's eye, saw the blue waters of the pool.

'Look, look,' demanded the cleaning lady. Miss Winter looked. The woman had mounted the low border between her balcony and the next. Her bulky silhouette balanced there for a fraction of a second and then dissolved in a glow of sunshine. Miss Winter closed her eyes. She was weary. She was weary with the effort of change and resolution. Her towel was still wedged tightly under her arm. She heard the waves, water racing past her feet. She opened her eyes.

'Now good,' exclaimed the cleaning lady, her bucket in one hand, her mop in the other. She had retrieved and rinsed a plastic mattress from the adjacent balcony, then placed it on a sunbed, where it dripped and glistened.

'Now good,' said the woman. 'Now you take sun.'

And she did.

Miss Winter lay in a world of dreams and rest and fantasy, caressed by distant voices from the promenade, safe in her secret balcony world. She needed no more than this. A giant step backwards for womankind? And what did she care?

'You have see the *Fantasia*?' asked the guide from the tour company as he drove her to the airport in his minibus.

Miss Winter was studying the wide vacant landscape, its flatness, its powdered brown earth. She was observing the men who stood by the roadside in their long beige and sludge-coloured robes, immobile, waiting and looking. Miss Winter had seen nothing. She looked at the guide.

'The wrong days,' she said. 'Next time.'

'Yes, next time,' said the guide. '*Insha'allah!*'

'Yes, *insha'allah,*' repeated Miss Winter.

They journeyed on smoothly, forward across this great expanse of road, splendid and untroubled. Miss Winter did not speak. She was absorbed. She was content. She was planning a holiday.

***

Black Sheep

The sheep were expensive because they were French. That's what Arthur told Mike and Chloe. The farmer harried the creatures roughly from the back of his pickup into Arthur's field. Six white, one black. Mike watched and counted, leaning on the corner of the porch, gripping a mug of tea in one hand.

'Those sheep are no more French than I am,' he said. 'Arthur said they cost 300. I'm betting Paulo charged him at least 450 a head.'

What Chloe wanted to say, but didn't, was, 'It takes a crook to spot a crook.'

'What's he going to do?' said Mike, 'Talk to them in French? *Comment allez-vous? Mon petit chou*, and all that? Do me a favour!' He took a gulp of his tea, then put down the cup and lit up a cigarette. 'What's wrong with Portuguese sheep then? Is he going to eat them? I don't think so. He'll keep them as pets and give them names.'

In the kitchen, Chloe turned the taps on full so she wouldn't hear his ranting. Everything was going to change because of those sheep. She knew it.

When they bought their *quinta* in this remote part of Central Portugal, Chloe hadn't imagined it would be like this. Sometimes she thought she hadn't made enough effort.

She'd put in the work at the beginning with the house, with the extended garden – a field really – and with Mike. Then, somehow, she'd run out of steam.

They'd made the purchase with their joint savings. Chloe wasn't entirely sure where Mike had got his. She didn't want to know. It was a fresh start for the two of them. Chloe was to be liberated from her social work. She wasn't cut out for it anyway. And she would take up her pen again or, at least, her laptop. Mike would begin anew with a clean slate, leaving behind his unpleasant memories of doing time in the Scrubs for theft and GBH. As if, thought Chloe, that injuring people was something to be forgotten.

Could, or would, Mike change? She told the Board that – yes – he had. But, as she knew very well, the potential for violence had always been there. There was no stopping Mike from losing it when he lost it. Chloe always forgave him for the bruises, and also for his drinking, his chain-smoking, his laziness, his mean spirit. She could deal with all of it. Her father had been guilty of most of those things. She had forgiven him too. Chloe had long wondered if men like these found her, or she found them. The social work, she realised, was one step too close to denial.

When they moved in, Mike and Chloe's only neighbours were a young couple with two children. Hearing their squeals of laughter, Mike grumped about them from the outset. Was it that he couldn't bear the pleasure of others? While he hissed and tutted, Chloe would watch the family wistfully from her kitchen window. It would have been reassuring in this foreign land to have at least a few friends at hand.

Though they gave no obvious clues, possibly the couple grew to dislike Mike as much as he despised them. The arrival of a massive removals van in their tiny country lane marked the end of their stay. The wife told Chloe that this return to the UK was part of a long-term plan, prompted by their concerns for elderly parents and the schooling of the children.

The For Sale sign went up but, not long after – to Mike's dismay – it came back down again. He would have had the place defy purchase and fall into disrepair. Now his best-case scenario was that the new owner would turn out to be an idle, childless, alcoholic soulmate. Chloe half-hoped that too. Better to have Mike intoxicated on his own porch with a neighbour than two villages away with Bill, his off-the-grid caravan-dwelling best mate.

Mike's dislike for the new owners and their university-aged offspring was almost instantaneous. Arthur and Lilian were know-alls, old, boring, snobbish. He would have had a go at the teenagers – layabouts, privileged, arrogant – but for the fact that they had headed back to university just a few weeks after their arrival. Was there anything or anyone, thought Chloe, that Mike ever had a good word for?

Mike's first disagreements with Arthur were about boundaries, and about the ownership of some of the trees that divided their land. They had words over the fallen fruit, the nectarines, the pears, the grapes that Arthur claimed were his, but that dangled over Mike's side of the border fence.

Mike monitored his neighbours' activities, watching them obsessively from the lounge window. Chloe would await with dread his introductory comment.

'You know,' said Mike, 'I see no improvements to that house from where I stand.' There would be a pause. Then, 'What's he up to now?' Mike would take a drag of his cigarette and say, 'I think it's time to nip out and take a look.'

And Chloe would say 'Don't.'

That morning, aided by Lilian, Arthur was drilling holes in fence supports.

Under his breath Mike said, 'Mind your fingers, Lilian. One slip of that drill and you're going to end up with a set of little stubs.' He picked up his mug and stepped outside. 'Morning, Arthur,' he said.

Chloe followed him to the porch, as she often did, preparing for an exercise in damage limitation.

Arthur looked up and grimaced. 'Watch out for that cigarette end, won't you?' he said.

Mike smiled, held the dog-end between his nicotine-stained fingers, then dropped it and ground it into the earth with his heel.

'Forest fires,' said Arthur.

'I know,' said Mike. 'Not going to stop me though, is it?'

'I don't know. Isn't it?' said Arthur.

Mike shrugged and walked back across the porch and into the house.

Chloe smiled, grew flushed, and followed him back inside.

Mike disliked the noise made by Arthur and Lilian's sheep – their French sheep. Chloe wondered how he even heard them when he played his music so loudly. He also complained about the cackling of the chickens, those same chickens that seemed to drop like flies. They'd know another chicken had gone when they saw Arthur and Lilian excavating a hole in the field even before the morning mist was up. The couple were back and forth constantly to the market to buy replacements. It crossed Chloe's mind that Mike had jinxed them with his hateful thoughts. Such was the power that she attributed to him in her darkest moments.

'There you go,' said Mike. 'They'd have us think they're experts, and they can't even keep a couple of chickens safe from the foxes. And what are they doing? Burying dead chickens under the woodpile and replacing them with new chickens like we'd never notice.'

Later that morning, Mike, feigning a stroll, passed Arthur as he worked on the repair of his boundary fence.

'Chickens all right then?' said Mike.

'Yes,' said Arthur.

'Heard a few squawks last night.'

'Right,' said Arthur.

'Just saying.'

Chloe heard it all, just as she saw the expression on Arthur's face, the clenched jaw. Anyone else would have been dreadfully provoked.

'You can't leave it alone, can you?' she said when Mike came back into the house. He got a beer from the fridge, popped the cap, then flung himself onto the sofa and switched on the TV.

'The silence of the chickens,' said Mike. 'What lies beneath the woodpile…'

'Did you do that?' said Chloe.

'What?' said Mike.

'Let those chickens out.'

'What do you take me for?' said Mike.

She thought, '*A criminal. I take you for a criminal,*' and as she thought that, she felt she was being disloyal and had betrayed him. She did not want to believe he was now everything she had fought to disprove.

In Arthur, for all his mildness, Chloe sensed a willfulness. While it irritated her, it antagonized Mike. Still, she could not understand why anyone would so despise people they hardly knew. This was what she could not fathom about Mike. It was as though all the resentment that he had rounded up and buried since his prison years had now resurfaced more violently than before.

'What is it with Arthur?' she asked him.

'What is what with Arthur?' said Mike.

'I don't understand why you hate him so much. What's he ever done to you?'

'Bloody hell,' said Mike, and he stared at the TV screen.

From the window, Chloe watched the sheep. She liked to watch the one black sheep, its head bobbing in amongst the white ones.

'You can't see it, can you?' said Mike. 'How mean he is. You don't know people the way I know people. You think everyone's good. I can tell you… they're not.'

'I'll make you a sandwich,' said Chloe. What she saw was this. Not that the reformed Mike had begun to revert back, but that he had never been anyone but himself. She hadn't been disloyal to him. *He* had misled *her*. There had only ever been one Mike.

From the lounge he shouted, 'Not chicken. Don't fancy chicken.'

Mike detested Lilian as much as he did Arthur. At the kitchen window, his first cigarette of the day hanging loosely between his lips, he'd watch as Lilian pushed her wheelbarrow down the lane, or as she carried her overgrown lettuces into the house. Pouring his coffee, he'd mutter, 'Stupid bitch.' Or he'd say, 'Gawd! What does she think she's wearing?' Then he'd say to Chloe, 'Why haven't you got any green wellies?' or 'See that? You're going to end up looking like that.' He'd scratch his unshaven chin, and say, 'I'll buy you some wellies, if you like. Green ones.' And then he'd snigger and choke on his cigarette. It could be endearing sometimes. Or used to be.

'Then there's her cooking,' said Mike. 'I don't know what the hell they eat over there. Whatever it is, I don't like it. I have to sit here while her dinner wafts over here into my house.'

'Our house,' said Chloe.

'Eh?' said Mike.

Chloe herself did have issues with Lilian which she dared not mention to Mike for fear of adding fuel to his loathing of the both of them. The more Mike raged on about Arthur, the more Chloe found fault in Lilian. Talking to her was like getting blood out of a stone. It seemed to Chloe that Lilian pitied her for not fulfilling her role of earth mother, clearing the land, pruning and tending the plants.

She would make unelicited statements about Chloe's patch of land. She would tell her that this tree or that would soon need cutting back. She would comment on plants that were underwatered or, worse still, not make comments, just step onto Chloe's land, examine a shrub, open her lips as if to speak, then say nothing but shake her head. The subtext was that these plants were in a desperate state. They were practically beyond hope because of Chloe's neglect, and would likely die unless Chloe were to ask Lilian to step in and save them.

But Chloe wanted nothing from Lilian. She did not want Lilian to save her or her plants. As she saw it, Lilian had a picture of how her neighbours should behave, and Chloe and Mike did not fit the frame. Chloe found it bad enough trying to keep Mike in line without having to deal with this constant provocation of Lilian's.

Chloe's irritation with Lilian's behavior was becoming something else entirely. Such was Mike's influence that she asked herself if this was really her, or Mike? She could not tell. She felt only that she could no longer abide that flabby face of Lilian's with its blob of country blush on either cheek, her jaw line lost in her neck. Chloe's abhorrence of Lilian's appearance was apprehension of the future. In this Mike had succeeded. As much as she had always intended to be her own person, Mike had molded and manipulated her, infiltrating and directing her beliefs about herself. The longer she stayed here, she was in danger of becoming another Lilian.

'I know what you're thinking,' said Mike, as the two of them viewed Lilian at work in her vegetable patch.

'What am I thinking?'

He nodded towards Lilian's splayed bottom, then sniggered and walked away. From the lounge, he shouted, 'How many pounds have you put on since we've been here then?'

And yet, Chloe couldn't see Mike morphing into another Arthur. Ever.

What Chloe did believe, however much it irked her, was that when you are miles from civilization and have no friends, you need to keep your neighbours on your side.

It was the business of the sheep that accelerated the enmity between Mike and Arthur. Chloe had hoped it wouldn't but suspected it might.

'What's he up to now? Him and his French sheep. He doesn't get it, does he? That he's been done.' Mike, as always, lingered at the kitchen window, watching through the gauze curtains.

'You're like an old lady,' said Chloe.

'Oooh!' said Mike, 'that's unacceptably sexist coming from someone like you.'

'Don't tell him that. About the sheep. You'll upset him,' said Chloe.

But he did. He went outside and he told him.

'Yes, they were expensive,' said Arthur. 'But they *are* a quality breed. That's what I paid for.'

'Well, just thought I'd mention it,' said Mike.

'Didn't you see how red he went when you said that to him?' said Chloe.

'Not my problem,' said Mike.

'Yes, I know it's not your problem. I'm just saying.' But she didn't say any more after that. It was another sighting of the alien inside this man. The alien she was sharing her life with. She had always given him the benefit of the doubt and, in the early days, her decisions had proved correct, but these last four years had been a period of regression. What if the change in Mike were down to her, a product of her boredom, her unfulfilled expectations, her desire for him to conform, and curb his unruly self? The self that had lain dormant.

Between them, of late, there were continued silences and miscommunications. His fault or hers? When Mike was away at Bill's – if indeed he was at Bill's – Chloe poured herself a glass of wine and watched the sheep. In her mind, the black sheep was hers. He was something special, different. The others were runts by comparison. That was what attracted her to him. She would look out and search for him and think, 'How's my black sheep today?'

She cared for him as if he were her own expensive French sheep. So, when she saw him limp across the grass evidently in pain, she could not but comment on it to Lilian.

'We had him sheared,' said Lilian. 'Paulo's friend did it. Five euros a sheep.'

'He messed up,' said Chloe.

Lilian assumed the look of the affronted. 'No, I don't think so. That often happens,' she said. 'Apparently.'

'Apparently, sheep can die if they get infected wounds,' said Chloe.

Lilian, in the manner of her husband, grew mottled and red around her plump, exposed neck.

'You need to get the vet in,' said Chloe. 'Give him a shot. Some antibiotics.'

'Oh,' said Lilian, looking up at the sky, 'was that a sparrowhawk?'

This feeling pity for the odd ones out, the outcasts, the underprivileged, this was Chloe's flaw – always feeling sorry for the black sheep. Especially when the black sheep was hurt. It wasn't as if she didn't know it. She indulged herself so as to justify her failings. And now she wanted to bestow her love on the black sheep, to care for it, to redeem and save it.

As the days passed, it continued to limp badly. The sheep was not getting better, but worse, and she was incapable of helping it. Did these people know anything at all about animals? They knew just about everything else. And Lilian was like a blank-eyed half-wit, staring through her when they met in the lane, daring her to make a comment. This was what she disliked about Lilian, the way she could clam up, and control you with her silence. This much Chloe knew, that if an animal was ailing, you got help immediately. Did Lilian think that the animal was going to heal itself?

In her preoccupation with the sheep, the issues with Mike assumed a lesser importance. When he became belligerent, she would leave him alone. More often than not, he slept in the spare bedroom.

She hadn't intended to bring up the subject of the injured sheep, but after two glasses of wine, late one evening while Mike was watching the football, it popped out. She couldn't stop herself.

'What did you expect?' said Mike. 'They know it all. They know how to kill a sheep.'

'I hope not,' said Chloe.

'You hope not,' said Mike, mimicking her. His latest gripe was about the chainsawed logs that Paulo had left by the fence separating their land. 'That wood is mine,' said Mike. 'Arthur says it's his. From his trees.'

'Maybe it is,' said Chloe, 'or maybe some of it's his and some is yours.'

'He's got a flipping woodpile that he's going to burn. He's got plenty of wood. He's so fucking bloody-minded. Don't you get it?'

'No,' she said. 'I don't.'

'Well, thank you for your support,' said Mike.

As he walked away, she heard him cussing under his breath. 'Don't swear at me,' she said.

'I'm going to Bill's,' he said.

'This late?'

'Piss off!' he said. He picked up his car keys and went outside, slamming the door behind him.

'Shit,' said Chloe, but before she could be the martyr and smash a glass or scream or throw a chair across the room, he came back.

'That fucking creep! He's parked his car right behind mine. I can't get out, can I?'

'Everything is effing this and effing that!' she said. 'For God's sake, leave it alone.'

'Yeah, that's your solution to everything. Leave it alone. Don't make a fuss.' He stood for a moment staring at her. Something in his look, in his eyes, changed.

In that split second, she thought, '*He's going to hit me.*'

Then he said simply, 'I'm going.'

She said, 'What?' She followed him into the bedroom and watched as he pulled a holdall from the wardrobe and, in silence, started to fill it with shirts, jeans, underwear, shaving things.

'Mike?' she said.

He said nothing. She felt the air hot with his anger.

'Okay,' she said. 'Piss off yourself and go!' She walked back to the kitchen, opened a cupboard, removed the bottle of whisky, and poured herself a glassful. She was halfway through the second glass when she heard the door open and then close. She hissed a litany of blasphemy into the air and, this time, she *did* throw a chair across the room. A glass shattered. Outside, as she staggered down the hallway clutching the bottle, she heard the barking of dogs from the nearby houses, a car engine, voices. She locked the bedroom door behind her, closed the outer shutters, the windows, the curtains. She wanted isolation, silence, oblivion, escape. Everything had been a mistake. She wanted the erasure of her errors, a new beginning, a release.

In the morning all was silence inside the house. She made coffee for one, then went outside to drink it on the porch. She couldn't remember how long it was since she had done this, sit quietly and just listen to the birds, to the sheep, to the rustling of the leaves. She had lived so long in the din that Mike had created that she was sucked in now by an unexpected tranquility.

She thought, '*He'll be back.*' But she realised with a start that she would have preferred for him not to come back. This feeling she had now, this was what it was really like to be alone. She could live with this feeling.

She knew she should call Bill. This was the unspoken protocol. It was what would be expected of her. It would show she cared about Mike and she was concerned to know where he was and when he was coming home. It would show also that she was worried about being on her own, about being deserted. It was for these reasons she knew she would *not* call Bill.

It seemed fitting to her that one day Mike should leave like this under the cover of darkness. She asked herself if this was the end of the relationship. If she had sensed an end to it, then so must he. Could she not live here alone? The Chloe of before had been ambitious and resourceful. Now she was a woman turned outside in, with her thoughts and plans hidden and lost within her. He had done that to her, but worse than that… she had let him do that to her. She had once believed a man would complete her and that, as a woman alone, she was not finished, not whole. She now knew that not to be true. Transposed to a different location, Mike had become the person he had always been. Transposed to a different location, *she* had become the person she had never been.

Chloe believed she was owed her isolation as a reward for those four years of self-sacrifice. She had had to have her freedom taken from her in order to appreciate its value. Whereas before her desire was to travel unburdened by possessions or people, now she found she wanted to enjoy what she never truly had been able to enjoy while Mike was there. The shared happiness had been an illusion. He shared nothing. He took. Such had been her love that she had stood in his shadow hoping to be absorbed by it. The shadow had transformed into a long dark night.

Through the rest of the morning, there were no calls and no texts. Chloe re-established order in the kitchen, a slightly damaged chair back in its rightful place, broken glass carefully packaged in the rubbish bin alongside an empty whisky bottle. All vague memories from the night before. She made herself a sandwich. If she was good at anything, she was good at making sandwiches. And, in the afternoon, she slept, waking much later to sun streaming through the window and the distant bleating of the sheep.

That day and those that followed marked a change in the pattern of her life. She walked the forest paths in the mornings, and ate breakfast late or not at all. In the afternoons, she relaxed on the porch, read a book, drank a glass of wine. Her phone remained silent. He was not going to say he was sorry. Nor was she. Without the car, she was inconvenienced, but it gave her an excuse to hike up the hill to the local shop, and to take a coffee and a cake at the bar next door. She would sit outside with her shopping, watching the villagers come and go, greeting her in this language she hardly knew. She asked herself why she had never done this before.

She saw little or nothing of her neighbours. Who could blame them for lying low with embarrassment following the parking debacle? Mike's absence now said it all. When she thought of Mike, her skin prickled, and her mouth went dry. If she were to hear the car return, if she were to hear his voice announcing his arrival, she would have felt dismay and disappointment. More than that. She would have felt anger.

When she dreamed, and she did so a good deal, she often dreamed of the black sheep. Her dreams were ineffable, dark. She saw tracks leading in many directions through the forest. She would be lost and then emerge in a shopping centre. She would open and close doors in a frenzied attempt to find her home, which meanwhile was inhabited by people she had never seen before, all of them friends of Mike. And, in her dream, she would awake to find the black sheep, shaggy with soil and insects and vermin, curled inside her blanket. This job of cleaning it was beyond her.

Looking out over the garden, she thought she might like to grow something. Despite the dreams but possibly because of them, she felt more tranquil than ever before. The idea of the earth coming alive and bringing forth goodness appealed to her. It would be something of hers, that she alone created and nurtured. Mike had never as much as pulled up a weed. He had laughed at her whenever she asked him to stop at a garden centre. She couldn't work at something that he willed to fail, so she had stopped asking. Since he left, she was a free agent. She could do as she pleased.

Chloe couldn't say exactly when it was that she noticed the absence of the black sheep. Her sheep. Returning from her walk, she stopped to watch the flock. The black sheep was not amongst them. Would Mike have stolen a sheep? He might have, but why? To spite Arthur perhaps. The thought seemed so absurd that she pushed it to the back of her mind. But if Mike had nothing to do with the sheep's disappearance, then something had happened to it. It had died through her neighbours' negligence. She hadn't given much heed to Mike's suggestion that Arthur and Lilian disappeared their mistakes under the woodpile, but when she passed the spot in the morning, she was certain that she could see freshly moved soil under the pruned tree branches.

When Chloe did see Arthur and Lilian, they were tight-lipped. They stared at her house through their car window as they drove in and out of the lane. When she passed them on her walks, they made no comment about their missing sheep. They made no comment about Mike's absence. Nor did Chloe. She and they were complicit in a kind of pretending.

And then it happened that instead of seeing Arthur and Lilian, she saw Paulo. He would drop by around midday, busy himself with the sheep, and rustle about around the chicken coop. Then he would sit on the back steps and drink a beer. Arthur and Lilian's car was gone. She didn't need to ask. This was their annual trip back home. They would be away a week or for as long as they could bear to leave their sheep, their chickens, and their home in Paulo's care.

Every day on her morning walk, Chloe passed the woodpile, and from the window of her lounge, in the distance she could see the mound of earth beneath it. If Mike had been there, he would have called her an idiot. Now she was alone and she could dare to do what she wanted. There was no one to tell her what she could or couldn't do.

That afternoon, Chloe waited until Paulo had finished his beer, locked the back door to the house, and driven away.

She crossed the lane, and let herself through the make-shift gate that closed off the corner of the field. She stared at the woodpile for what seemed like a very long time, the silence broken only by the bleating of the sheep and the cawing of crows. Then she pulled on her rubber gloves and set to work moving the branches.

When the area was cleared, she began to dig. As she worked, the sheep surrounded her and watched. The soil was rich and loose. As she dug and threw aside the earth, she was all too aware of the absurdity of the scene. There was insanity in her action, but she pressed on because it was illicit, because she wanted to know for sure if her imaginings had any basis. Her life and her decisions had been founded on instinct. And instinct, she knew now, took too long to affirm. Her neighbours had not told her about the black sheep, had not admitted to its fate. They had deceived her just as Mike had, but now she was in control of the resolution.

A surge of rank air, something evil-smelling, stopped her. She recoiled, staggered back, paused for breath, her face moist with sweat. She thought, '*This is it.*' She looked up at the sheep, and in their midst, its ghost eyes staring back at her, was one black sheep – her sheep. She looked down at the ground. There in the soil, she saw it. A human hand, decayed, slime-covered, the fingers like leather, the fingertips darkly yellowed. Nicotine-stained.

She kicked the soil back into place. All of it. With the toe of her boot. Stomping down the earth. Feverishly. The sheep scattering. She threw down the branches, sent them crashing onto the ground, went back at a half-run towards the house. Gasping to regain herself. The sheep bounded away as she passed. And it occurred to her that from here her house looked pretty, that anyone would want to buy this house, that she might ask Paulo to fence off the land, that she could keep sheep of her own, that they could be any colour, black or white.

Later, in her dream, she saw the black sheep. He was there with the rest of the flock. He had always been there. The sheep clustered together, a mess of shabby, curdled wool and then, in their midst, a smear of black.

***

Body Language

When was it that Fiona first noticed her body was changing? Exactly when, she couldn't remember. Very slight and very slow were the variations. But this she did recall, in that enslaving ritual, the putting on of make-up, one morning discovering long, silky hairs sprouting from her upper lip, waving, slithering their way out of the sides of her mouth, escaping. Viewing her face sideways on, other hairs she saw emerging like soft reeds from the pits of her skin, layering the surface with a delicate and unctuous mask as she coated them with foundation.

She was opposed at first to the beautician's removal of errant hairs. The expert advised an urgent repair to the face bared before her. For every hair removed, two would grow in its place. So said her mother, and soon Fiona would come to believe her. Mothers, necromancing, they always know. But there, you see, weeks passed with nothing happening. Until. Until in the place of every missing hair came harsh, black sprouts akin to the spikes in the beard of a man, perhaps even a little like the rough pelt of an animal, camouflaged, creeping with stealth from the forest behind her house.

And other changes came. Her toenails, previously clear and straight, grew hard and ridged, yellowing at the edges, elongating in the brief period that elapsed between one visit and another to the pedicurist, hooking over, tearing, wearing down her expectations. How should a woman address her body's needs? Soaking, scrubbing feet with diligence? Yet look how the yellowing extends to the face of each whole nail, how walking has become uncomfortable, how the toenails have curved in on themselves, how each toe has sawed at the next.

Surely, only if cures could be had without her exposing and betraying the body would a visit to the doctor be warranted. A nurse or medical practitioner, they might deduce this, or reduce this to body abuse, a lack of maintenance by a woman who reveled in narcissism, and whose Saturday pedicure, so perfect in execution was, by the Tuesday after, eliminated, such was the rate of growth and the shape they took, these talons, these claws.

To waken at night to the chafing and ripping of bedsheets, to waken to the excessive warmth of blossoming fur, to waken to the rarest of desires, incomprehensible, in both spirit and flesh. Who could not acknowledge the change this body demanded? Who could define the nature and intention of the change? Was blame to be attributed? No beast was there in her that she could see. For us all, there never is.

But, just a precaution, then, when waking in the morning, that we must pray after unnatural dreaming that all will again be normal and obey an urgency to check in the mirror to see what we may have become. Can we blame Fiona in her metamorphosis? Was she remiss in recognizing and challenging those sharpened eyes, the rusted malodorous incisors, the erect and bristling ears, the twitching nose, even now trembling and inhaling as, below, the young carpenter, at work on her kitchen shelves, misses a nail with his hammer, and draws blood?

***

Race Days

It was on one of the days when Tomasz was returning from the cemetery that he saw his dead brother on the bus. He could swear it was him. 'Same build, same hair, same ears, same everything,' he told Barbara.

'Why didn't you go and speak to him?' she said. 'If it had been me, I'd have wanted to take a closer look.'

'Oh no,' said her dad. 'I'd have missed my stop.'

'Well, I don't know about that,' said Barbara. 'It's not as if someone sees their deceased brother every day, is it?'

'What's "deceased"?' said Tomasz.

'Never mind,' said Barbara.

Tomasz was a solitary man, but a contented one. He had his own little rituals and routines, and that was the life he enjoyed. For five years, he had made the weekly visit to the cemetery to tidy his wife's grave. The way Barbara saw it, her mother was gone and visiting her grave wasn't going to change anything or repair their shared feelings of loss.

A day or so after the brother-on-the-bus incident, Tomasz came down to breakfast with his three-dreams story.

'I had three dreams about her,' he told Barbara.

'What kind of dreams?' said Barbara.

'Nice dreams,' he said, 'you know … about placing bets at the bookie's, and doing the cooking.'

'I don't suppose she'd have been thrilled about any of that, especially not the race days,' said Barbara. "What was the third dream?"

"I don't know," he said. "I can't remember."

Tomasz spent his mornings doing chores – things like shopping or going to the launderette – and he spent his afternoons watching TV in his bedroom. He could watch films over and over and be constantly amused since he never ever remembered that he'd seen them before. It was on one of those typical afternoons that the doorbell rang at a time when no one was expected.

'Who's that?' he asked Barbara. He always said, 'Who's that?' as though Barbara was some kind of clairvoyant. It was a race day and he was watching the horseracing from Newmarket. He liked a bit of a flutter, though he claimed otherwise.

Barbara picked up the door phone. 'Hello? Hello?' she said, but no one answered. 'I'll go down and take a look,' she told him, but he wasn't much bothered.

She ran down three flights of stairs and when she got to the corridor leading to the front door, she could see out onto the main road. Their front door was a mirror on the outside and see-through glass on the inside – useful for passersby who wanted to check their appearance or comb their hair. Barbara couldn't see anyone lingering outside in the road. She thought maybe she'd catch someone loping up the street, some kid taking a chance at ringing the doorbell for fun, or maybe an acquaintance who didn't think to wait, or a post office delivery van. Peering out, she saw only the street, for the most part empty, and the traffic passing – quite a lot of it. She looked first to the left and after that to the right … and then she saw it. The funeral procession.

There was a large black hearse, highly polished, moving slowly down the road. Walking in front of the car was the undertaker, completely in black, wearing a top hat and looking like something out of Dickens. Other limousines followed, and they contained the mourners. She couldn't see them clearly. She stood behind the glass and watched the cars pass, the procession holding up the weekday traffic, which moved bumper to bumper. She turned to go back upstairs but, as if doubting what she had seen, she returned to the door and looked again. The cortège had gone. Vanished. The traffic flowed freely.

When she returned upstairs and stepped back into the flat, Tomasz called out to her from his room.

'Who was it?' he said.

'No one,' she said.

Two days later, just as the horses in the 4:10 at Newmarket passed the winning post, Tomasz collapsed with a heart attack. Barbara tried to resuscitate him, helped by a woman from the emergency services who talked her through the steps over the phone. But Tomasz was dead on arrival at the hospital.

Barbara organised the funeral with – insurance policies permitting – no expense spared. Small and contained though his later life had been, she believed Tomasz deserved to have a memorable send off. She pushed away her grief until the arrangements were complete. Only then on the way to the cemetery, the sky fittingly overcast, did it seem to her as if she had at last fallen awake.

Looking about her, she saw that the cortège was taking exactly the same route as the funeral procession she had seen that afternoon just a week or so before. The Dickensian undertaker walked in front of the shiny black hearse, while Barbara sat in one of the limousines that followed on its tail. As they passed the front of her house, she saw the procession reflected in its mirrored door.

From where she sat, looking up at the building's façade, Barbara strained to see the flickering light in her father's upstairs window. It was, after all, a race day.

***

VISITOR

Nicola met a man on the plane when she was coming home to London from Zurich. She found him very pleasant. They talked at length during the journey. It seemed like they had a lot in common. She gave him her number and she invited him to visit the house in Bromley that she shared with her fellow students.

They were surprised and not a little curious that she was to have a guest. Up to then she had never invited anyone.

She told them, 'It's not a boyfriend. It's just a friend.'

And they said, 'That's okay. We get it.'

He came on a rainy Wednesday afternoon. He was glad to step inside from the cold. Everyone made him welcome. They sat him down in their best armchair and they gave him tea and biscuits. They chatted at length, and after an hour or so, he thanked them all for their hospitality and headed back to the station.

When he had gone, Nicola's Jamaican housemate asked her, 'Why didn't you tell us he was black?'

***

Gene-ius

1. Self-belief

Miranda is a smallish person, who knows everything with absolute certainty. Julie despises Miranda for her skin-care secrets, and everything else that she cannot quite put her finger on. Later in her life, Julie realises there will always be girls like this, who do not have strange-sounding foreign surnames, and who have everything going for them, including their skin. Miranda's skin is translucent, icy, and faintly bluish around her eye sockets. She believes she is striking, and self-belief fosters conviction in others. It disappoints Julie that her teachers and, in particular, Sister Myra, see a strikingness only in Miranda and not in her. Recognizing this, Julie attributes the lows in her life to Miranda, but also to her own unacceptable refu-genes.

2. A liberal education

Sister Myra tells the class that people should marry their own kind. It makes for disharmony and confusion when different sorts mix. Fay, Jamaican mother and English father, is in that class, as is Amira, Egyptian father and French mother, and then there is Stefania, Italian father and Scottish mother. But, as Sister Myra speaks these words, Julie knows they refer specifically to her, Polish father and English mother.

In later years when she is over this, she decides that Sister Myra must have been very conflicted. Miranda, Irish mother and Irish father, is in with a chance.

Rebecca Joseph does something bad. She does it in the bushes in the park. Which park and what exactly, Julie does not know, and no one is telling. She thinks the *park* may be somewhere in Hampstead and the *what* may be linked to the seven pages – 41 to 48 – removed from their Biology text-books. Julie is sorry that it is not Miranda who has been caught out, and that it is not Sister Myra who has caught her. People who should get caught, she concludes, aren't.

Sister Myra favours a liberal education. Freedom of speech, freedom of expression, freedom of worship, the welcoming of those of other faiths – Jews, Muslims, Hindus, Buddhists, and a few others she can never remember when she speaks of them in morning assembly. For Julie, it is good to know that she can go far in life if she keeps an open mind and is not a Protestant. Since Miranda has no refu-genes, the likelihood is that she will go much further.

3. Decision-making

On the day that Julie and her mother have their appointment with Sister Myra to discuss the decisions that will affect the next ten years of Julie's life, Julie's only ally – the diminutive Sister Frances – sneezes whilst walking down one of the convent's darkened corridors and knocks herself out on a holy statue, possibly that of St. Teresa. Sister Myra has insisted that the lights be dimmed to help reduce the sisters' electricity bill. Had Sister Frances been taller, her collision with the statue would have resulted in a blow to the upper chest instead of a clout to the head.

While she lies stunned on the parquet floor upstairs, downstairs in the Lower Sixth study room, Sister Myra tells Julie's mother that her daughter is not up to taking 'A' levels. Julie knows that Miranda isn't up to taking 'A' Levels either, though that does not seem to matter to Sister Myra.

4. Blame

After her marriage, it took Julie's mother two months to learn how to spell her new surname. Julie's friend Sarah says that to avoid a similar problem, Julie should think of marrying someone English, not a foreigner and especially not a refugee. Sarah herself isn't worried about the man's name, only about his feet. She can't abide men with small feet.

So, when Julie meets Simon at Sarah's birthday party, she looks long and hard at his shoes. She notes how Miranda also looks Simon over. His feet and his name are not important when, two months later, Miranda steals him from Julie at Stefania's birthday party. The questions for Julie are: Did Miranda steal him because she liked him, or did she steal him because she didn't want Julie to have him, or because Simon himself wanted to be stolen? Is Miranda the culprit, or is Simon the one at fault? Or is it all down to Julie herself? Which is probably what Sister Myra would have concluded.

5. Refu-genes

Andrew Kaczmarek also has refu-genes. His mother feeds him daily with boiled eggs, causing him to be both blocked and spotty. Mrs. Kaczmarek meets Julie's mother in the street and remarks that she is looking forward to the day when their children will return home to rebuild their country.

When mother and son have gone on their way, Julie asks, 'What country?'

To which her mother replies, 'Don't mind her. No one's going back anywhere. Not even your father.'

Andrew could have been a boyfriend, but not if he was intending to go back to some distant and unknown land. Julie sure as Hell wasn't going.

At junior school, during the playground wars, Julie stabs Jeremy in the cheek with an HB pencil. The stabbing is an accident, of course. Difficult to say if this is anything to do with the unpredictability of people with refu-genes.

After Andrew and Jeremy, there are grammar-school boys with big hair, painters, sculptors, holiday romances, medical students, and political science graduates. Somewhere in the middle of these, there is the Simon stolen by Miranda. In this period of her life, Julie suspects that her refu-genes contribute to her incompatibility issues.

6. Goals

When Dora says she fancies Father Donovan, Julie pays him some attention. She can't see it herself and wonders if that is the best Dora can do. Years later she thinks that this may be one of her personal failings, aiming too high, when instead she should take what is readily available, a fresh-faced boy from a family of impoverished intellectuals. Someone like Simon. While she knows she is outclassed because of her refu-genes, she also persuades herself that Simon was, in any case, not good enough for her, especially since he was so easily enticed away by Miranda.

Meanwhile, Dora, who never gets to sit her 'A' levels, runs away with Father Donovan. What they may have been running away from Julie cannot say. School and Sister Myra possibly. The 'running away' is how her mother describes it.

Miranda never runs away with anyone. She mostly takes and discards, Simon being a case in point. Julie never runs away with anyone either. She thinks that one day she might regret this.

7. Learning

School teaches Julie to play tennis and netball and rounders. She can scramble up a rope and bounce over a wooden horse. She can dance a polka and a waltz, and a miscellany of country reels in which she has dragged her partners under arches of skinny arms, and skipped sideways opposite girls with bouncy bosoms. She has learned her Catechism, but cannot remember it.

She can get by in French and German, and knows some Latin but not Greek, because Greek is for boys and not for girls. She knows about Caesar's *Gallic Wars*, the French Revolution, and the Unification of Italy. She pities Luther because, rather like Andrew Kaczmarek, he is constipated and has a troubled mind, maybe even spotty.

From Jane Austen, Julie learns that Darcy is a misery and will remain so, and that no woman can change a man who won't be changed. Julie has also read *Persuasion* and understands something of another woman's mind. Not Sister Myra's. But then Sister Myra isn't a woman as such. Nor is Sister Myra the sort to be admiring the way someone has learned useless skills. Unless it happens to be Miranda.

8. Assimilation

At university, Julie puts school and Miranda and Simon and Sister Myra behind her. At the Students' Union Saturday night disco, she dances with two male acquaintances at the same time. One is Greg Hughes, the lab tech, whose girlfriend looks uncannily like Miranda. The other is Julie's History tutor Michael Brigham-Wright, a figure of some authority. Hughes and Brigham-Wright repair to the delivery bay at the rear of the building and, against the odds, Brigham-Wright slugs Hughes in the jaw and then gives him a black eye. They settle out of court and Brigham-Wright makes a generous contribution to a charity of Hughes' choosing.

Oblivious to this incident, Julie leaves the disco that night with Xavier the Jamaican lithographer from Balham and goes to see his etchings. She also views many other artworks in the course of her university life. Her refu-genes, she feels, now aid her assimilation into a changing world.

9. Career

Hired, post-university, by Caroline – a slight resemblance there to Miranda – Julie rises through the ranks to the level of middle manager, thus finding her corporate self. She discovers that she dislikes wimpled women. When, first, Fatima from Royal Holloway and then Leyla from Manchester apply for posts as junior sales executives within Julie's department, she gives the job to neither of them. Instead, she chooses Marcus, who fetches and carries for her, and who brings her the contents of Caroline's wastepaper basket every day at close of business. After six months in the company, Julie replaces Caroline as Head of Marketing. Benefits: car, company credit card, business-class foreign travel, and miscellaneous perks. Marcus, she sees now, reminds her too much of Simon – previously lost to Miranda – so she has to let him go.

10. Perspective

Endings are for stories, not for life, except, of course, for death. Of Simon's end, Julie doesn't much care. He is not the issue, she understands now. She understands too that she can only guess at endings, or at least not be disappointed by expecting them. Perhaps they can be predetermined if the likes of Sister Myra have anything to do with them. Who is to say if going back is an act of masochism or a statement of achievement, a look-at-me-I-wasn't-good-enough-for-'A'-levels kind of return? The Mirandas of this world go back, but what of the Julies? They are ready to help their story along, ready to be flipped upside down and to see the world from another perspective. Not such a bad idea to change the picture now and then. To twirl destiny around.

11. Achievements

Julie drives a black limo. Car phone, SatNav, leather upholstery. Refu-genes made good. Gene-ius. This is how she has always imagined she should return to the convent.

Sister Frances, bent, blank-eyed, and predictably withered, with the faintest of scars on her forehead, ushers her into Sister Myra's empty sitting room. There are papers and letters on a desk in the corner, a travelling alarm clock on the mantelpiece, a photo album on a coffee table. The room is heated by a gas fire, but there is a musky, damp smell in the air, of things old and decayed, of memories Julie no longer cares to remember.

Seated in one of two worn armchairs, Julie examines the photos. The faces are altered but still recognisable, mature women, with tinted hair, Botoxed faces, CEO husbands, handbags, grown-up children, Chihuahuas, ageing in-laws, designer labels, houses in Surrey and Spain, responsibilities. All have turned out as anticipated.

Julie flips a page. The door opens.

12. Great expectations

Sister Myra is older, softly wrinkled, plumper, but essentially the same. She has that look that continues to tell Julie that she has disappointed.

'It's Miranda,' says Sister Myra. 'Do you see?'

Julie looks down, and yes, there she is, preserved under cellophane. Miranda, who never aspired to 'A' Levels, who is now the image of all the others.

Life is about stories. A story is a metaphor, and the metaphor means something to you deep down in your dark flowing river of a subconscious. If the story is a good one, it will take you with it over the oceans of memory and belief. If it is a bad one, for the rest of your life you will wonder where you went wrong, and if your genes might have been the cause.

'And who would have thought,' says Sister Myra, 'that Miranda would have done so well for herself in life?'

***

Times Tables

The two Mr Timpsons taught times tables. Their pupils thought well of them. The girls, for it was so in those days, considered one Mr Timpson more handsome than the other. The boys regarded both Mr Timpsons as tough and heroic. It was difficult to distinguish the first Mr Timpson from the second. One Mr Timpson taught English, the other football. They both taught times tables.

It was rumoured that one of the Mr Timpsons – probably the second – had a glass eye.

'Definitely his right eye,' swore Jolyon. 'It's bigger than the left.'

'I think it's his left eye,' countered Patsy. 'It shines when the light's on.'

'You're stupid,' said Jolyon, with a scowl. And thus the discussion would end.

Immersed in a world of dreams and television and playground ambitions, sprawled across her desk with her head propped vertically against one straining elbow, Patsy would focus speculation around the second Mr Timpson's eyes. It could be the left, but there again it could be the right. They might even both be glass.

'Now, if you all behave yourselves,' announced the second Mr Timpson, 'we'll have our first pen and ink lesson on Thursday.'

Uproar ensued.

In the milk break, Jolyon took the opportunity to explain the connection between Mr Timpson's glass eye and the pen and ink lesson.

'Someone stuck a nib in his eye,' he said to his horrified audience.

David turned puce, spat out his straw, and squealed.

'That's why...' continued Jolyon, making sure that everyone understood, 'that's why he tells us off when we wave our arms about. We might stick a pen in someone's eye. But, not Christopher's,' he added, 'because he wears glasses.' He scanned the group. 'But maybe...' he said, 'maybe David's, because he doesn't.' David squealed again, imagining a pen in an eye, like Excalibur in a stone. They all looked at Christopher and considered how fortunate was his lot in life.

Patsy was not so much concerned with pens and nibs as she was with times tables. Perhaps it would be her turn this week, she thought. She was sure Mr Timpson, whichever Mr Timpson he was, would not forget her.

'It's my turn to do the times tables this week,' she said.

Jolyon's lip curled, and he threw his milk bottle in the crate. 'You''re stupid,' he said, and walked away.

'Now, whose turn is it to be our conductor today?' asked one of the two Mr Timpsons, surveying the room with one normal eye and one glassy eye. A sea of arms shot up, stretching and reaching before him. Children hurled themselves bodily across desks.

'Me, Mr Timpson, me, Sir, me,' came the cry.

'It's my turn, Mr Timpson,' shouted Patsy, but her voice was tiny and distant.

Mr Timpson stood majestically before his subjects as a king granting petitions. Whose dreams would he fulfil today, whose ambitions, whose temporary glory would he grant in his magnanimity? Who would enter the playground triumphant this lunchtime, and be forever in his debt? In his grandeur and omnipotence, he forgot the likes of Patsy.

'Jolyon,' he said, and beamed a glassy radiance.

Jolyon grinned, looked about him and came to the front of the class. He was still grinning as he took the baton. The class fell silent. It was a time for reverence, a moment of most sublime magic. Jolyon wiped his nose quickly on his sleeve, hitched up his drooping flannel shorts, and held the stick high in the air. He was imperious. The children dared not breathe. And then he began, like the magician he believed he was.

'*One seven is seven. Two sevens are fourteen.*'

They chanted.

'*Three sevens are twenty-one.*'

He pointed the wand. An incantation.

'*Four sevens are twenty-eight.*'

From one row to the next. Rhythmically. No hesitations.

'*Five sevens are thirty-five.*'

A mistake would be dishonour, and Jolyon pointed.

'*Six sevens are forty-two.*'

His arm flicked left, then right.

'*Seven sevens are forty-nine*' they had to be on their toes '*eight sevens are fifty-six,*' faster '*nine sevens are sixty-three*' too fast more difficult now '*ten sevens are seventy*' they had to think hard '*eleven sevens are seventy-seven*' their row might be next they were out of breath. '*Twelve sevens are eighty-four.*'

Their voices stopped abruptly. The resonance stayed ringing and vibrating in the air around them.

'Well done,' said Mr Timpson as Jolyon threw down the wand and swung himself from desk to desk, dangling his skinny mud-splattered legs in the air – Tarzan of the desktops – until he bounced back into his chair. The grin stayed. He looked about him to receive the adulation of his companions.

'Well done, boys and girls,' said Mr Timpson. 'We'll do the eight times table next,' and then the bell jingled and jangled in their ears. 'You can go now,' he shouted above the riot.

'*One eight is eight. Two eights are sixteen.*' Patsy could live with disappointment. Mr Timpson might choose her next time, she thought. She saw the class before her obedient and reverent, their concentration, Jolyon''s envy, the baton in her raised hand, poised for that first gesture of command.

'We'll have a quarter of ham, half a dozen eggs and a pound of sugar,' said Patsy's mum. Patsy stood pressing her nose up against the glass, trying to see something that inspired her amongst the cold meats.

'Do you fancy some sausages for your tea?' said her mother.

Patsy screwed up her face. She'd eaten yesterday and at lunchtime today. Now she had to do it all over again.

'Don't be like that,' said her mother, and bought half a pound of sausages.

'Studying hard, are you?' said Phyllis, the lady from the cake shop.

'Yes,' whispered Patsy, and gazed in fascination as Phyllis created a box from a sheet of thin white card.

'I wish I was clever,' said Phyllis.

Patsy watched entranced as Phyllis lifted the cakes swiftly and expertly into the box and tied it with a length of shiny yellow tape.

'Of course, it'll have to stop,' said Phyllis.

Phyllis always said that. What had to stop? Patsy didn't know, and didn't care. The words floated over her head. Phyllis lowered the box down to her.

'Don't eat them all in one go now,' she warned. 'See you next Friday.'

Back in the street, Patsy bounced the box on its string and let the cakes bump and slide within. She would lick the cream off the inside of the box when they got home.

'Don't do that, love,' said her mother. 'The cream'll stick to the sides of the box.'

It was dark now, people scurrying home to escape the cold. Across the road, the bombsite was faintly illuminated like a distant stage, on which there walked three characters of varying height.

'Those boys are always up to something,' said her mother.

Jolyon led his silhouetted troupe across the bricks and rubble. Jolyon, then Simon, then Keith. They whistled as they skipped and jumped, one behind the other.

'Look at them!' said Patsy's mother.

Patsy frowned and manoeuvred the cake box from her left hand to her right, and the shopping bag from her right to her left. She envied Jolyon the freedom of his world.

The bombsite looked different on a Sunday morning. The sun glinted on the cement mixers and ladders. It sent crooked brick-shaped shadows across scaffolding and wooden planks. Patsy could not imagine there would be buildings here. She liked it as it was.

'Fresh air,' said her father, inhaling deeply as the traffic trundled past. It was a far cry from Kilburn. 'The air's much better at Notting Hill Gate,' he said, turning from the wind to shelter his face and light a cigarette. Patsy couldn't really comment. She hadn't a lot to compare it with.

On Tuesday morning Mr Timpson, the first Mr Timpson, did not come to class.

'He's dead,' said Jolyon, bouncing up and down on his chair. 'We'll have to go to his funeral.'

'Is he? Is he?' squealed David, his face turning red and congested.

Mr Steele entered the room, surveying his property. 'Now pay attention,' he said. 'The two Mr Timpsons will be away for a few days. Miss Singh will be taking your class.'

Miss Singh, in green sari with red trim took her place at Mr Timpson's desk. Mouths fell open, elbows nudged and dug. Grinning and leering, Jolyon bounced on his weathered chair. Miss Singh eyed him with suspicion.

'The boy in the fourth row,' she said. 'Do you want to be excused?'

Jolyon froze, merging with the environment.

'Yes, you,' she said fixing him, the huntress with her bow. 'Do you want to go to the bathroom?'

Rose spluttered giggles. Simon's shoulders vibrated. Keith opened his desk and put his head inside.

'No,' said Jolyon.

'No, Miss Singh,' she corrected.

All eyes were now on Jolyon. Keith peeped above his desktop.

'No, Miss Singh,' said Jolyon.

'In that case,' said Miss Singh, 'please stop fidgeting. If you wish to go to the bathroom,' she said, casting her all-seeing eye around the class, 'put up your hand and say, "Please, Miss Singh, may I go to the bathroom?" Is that clear?'

'Yes, Miss Singh,' chanted the chorus.

There was little joy to be had with Miss Singh. The children fell into a profound silence. Looks were exchanged from behind desktops.

'The girl in row two. Have you lost something?'

'No, Miss Singh,' said Patsy.

'In that case,' said Miss Singh, 'you can close your desk.'

'Are we going to do the times tables today, Miss Singh?' asked Patsy.

The children were dumbstruck at Patsy's nerve. Miss Singh shuffled papers, looking for instructions. Like spectators at a tennis match, the children's eyes moved from Patsy to Miss Singh. Would she concede this point, they wondered?

'Very good,' said Miss Singh. 'Today we shall do the times tables. The eight times table.' She studied the class.

'It's my turn today, Miss Singh,' Patsy piped in her thin voice.

Miss Singh looked over the top of her glasses. 'You shall have your chance later,' she said. 'The boy in the third row,' she continued, catching David's eye hypnotically, 'please stand up.'

David stood, growing scarlet.

'Now, tell me,' she said, 'what are three eights?'

David stared, speechless, at Miss Singh.

The class gasped. These were not the times tables as they knew them. Jolyon scowled in Patsy's direction.

The following Monday, Mr Timpson, one of the two, was back at his desk. His father had died. Mr Steele told the class they were to be very good. Patsy studied Mr Timpson, looking for changes. His father was dead, but he looked just as he did before.

'I think it's time for the times tables,' said Mr Timpson. He caught Patsy off guard.

'It's my turn, Mr Timpson,' she shouted weakly. But Mr Timpson had already made his choice.

'Jolyon,' he said. 'Come and conduct us. Quickly,' he said as Jolyon lingered, grinned and enjoyed admiration.

Patsy was angry. '*One nine is nine. Two nines are eighteen.*' Her mother was right. This was a case of the one Mr Timpson not knowing what the other Mr Timpson was doing. '*Three nines are twenty-seven.*' Jolyon had had two goes. She hadn't even had one. '*Four nines are thirty-six.*' Maybe Mr Timpson couldn't count. '*Five nines are forty-five,*' and Jolyon should have told Mr Timpson that he'd already had his go.

'You're on our side of the playground,' Patsy shouted as Jolyon wove his bomber in and out of the skipping ropes. The girls screamed and jumped aside as the rest of the squadron followed. '*Six nines are fifty-four,*' she thought bitterly.

Jolyon was unprepared for the counterattack. His entire command was in enemy territory. The enemy was in his. It was a strategic dilemma. There was a violent swarming of forces back and forth across the border. There were pushes and shoves and shouts and tears, boys strangled with skipping ropes, girls hit by footballs. Mrs Brown, the playground monitor, had not coped with a war before. She waddled towards the centre of the conflict like an uncertain fly towards an electric fan. She was mangled.

'Jolyon,' said Mr Steele. 'My office. Now.'

Mr Blake, the school-keeper, tended Patsy's knee. As he searched for bandages, she sipped a cup of hot, syrupy tea and scrutinised the gravy trail from her knee to her blood-stained sock. Wounded in the line of duty. Heroism was made of this.

'All in one piece,' said Mr Blake, smiling as he consigned her to Mr Timpson. She had missed most of Tuesday morning. Mr Blake had let her read his *Daily Express*.

Seeing Patsy's pale face, the huge bandage and the bloodied sock, Mr Timpson's heart softened.

'Patsy, I think it's your turn today.'

Her knee tingled and stung. She had fought for this moment. She stood before the class, the baton in her hand held high, a moment of exquisite glory. Already she could hear the chant vibrating in her ears—

And then the bell rang. The lesson was ended. The children flew from their seats.

'Sorry, Patsy,' boomed Mr Timpson amidst the chaos. 'Next time.'

Patsy limped from the classroom.

'Time for the times tables,' said Mr Timpson on Friday morning. Ten did not challenge Patsy as much as nine. She rose from her seat, her heart pounding.

'David!' said Mr Timpson.

'But it's my turn,' said Patsy.

Jolyon stood up and swung between the desks.

'Sit down, Jolyon,' said Mr Timpson. 'You had your go last time, Patsy. It's David's turn today.'

Jolyon smirked in Patsy's direction, bouncing on his weary chair. It creaked and groaned and wobbled. Then, quite without warning, Jolyon slid beneath the desks, as if sucked from below by a marauding shark. Patsy caught sight of his startled face as, soundlessly, he disappeared from view.

And there he should stay, thought Patsy. Such is the bitterness and the injustice provoked by the times tables.

*

At the greengrocer's, David was working out her bill.

'What's nine sevens?' he asked, licking the end of his pencil.

'You ought to know,' said Patsy.

David grew red. 'Come on,' he said.

'Sixty-three,' sighed Patsy. She was in a hurry. She got into her car. '*Nine sevens are sixty-three*,' she thought, and she started the engine. '*Ten sevens are seventy.*' She had to collect the children from school and get their tea. '*Eleven sevens are seventy-seven.*' And Jolyon's supper. '*Twelve sevens are eighty-four.*'

***

Snow Garden

In the square behind Laura's flat, there is a garden. She can see it from her kitchen window. It is surrounded by a high wire grill, painted olive green. Behind the grill, she can see hedges, dense shrubbery, and the passing colours of people's clothes, the pastel jumpsuits of infants and, streaking past, the glossy, groomed coats of well-tended pets.

In the summer she can hear the biff-baff of tennis balls and the shouts of the players. There are other voices too: young women chattering, the dark laughter of men, the squeals of children. Then, in winter, the garden becomes silent and still. Creatures dart behind the olive grill, blacknesses blot the snow, birds tip into patches of gloom beneath the iced branches. But, beyond the fence, all is a mass of undefined white. Dazzling and immobile.

She is in the street, on the snow-covered pavement, on the outside of the meshwork. There is no distinction between pavement and road. The white is spread evenly across the undulating surfaces, flaws are masked, carpeted white. She has defined her game. She is making a snowman. There is no one to say this is right or wrong, or you do it this way, not that. This is something entirely of her own making. She has seen it done and now she is applying herself. She rolls a snowball, turns it creaking in the white fluff. It grows as it rolls. It turns heavily. She pushes it, coaxes it across uncharted expanses so it becomes huge and enviable.

There is a thud. She looks up to the trees. Something has fallen. Her attention is on the boulder that she is pushing before her. Another thud. She looks around her. Something smashes at her feet. She looks down, bemused. A snowball. There is movement behind the fence, a dark figure, a boy hurling snowballs. Today his name escaped her, yet she must have known it then.

He is imprisoned on the inside of the wire fence. He is locked inside his huge cell of a garden and longs to come out. She is on the outside and longs to go in, for there are, surely, delights in there that she cannot even imagine.

That was then. Years later, after her mother had died, she thought to ask the local administrator if she and her father could use the gardens.

"You do understand," the woman told her, "that there's a waiting list.'

Yes, Laura did understand.

'Write to me, then," said the woman. "I'll put you on the list."

So, she wrote the letter. And, after that, she waited.

Laura was in the street, treading carefully on the snow-covered pavement, where there was no distinction between pavement and road. But now she was old – almost as old as her parents were then. These days there was no need to make a snowman, and whatever delights there were in the garden, she had long since imagined and forgotten them.

***

LOST FOR WORDS

That year, it was not yet the season for voice loss, but Fay had lost hers. First, she said, there was a frog in her throat, then she became a little hoarse, and very soon a whole menagerie seemed to have spirited away that 'voice' in her voice. The doctor, she said, had been all for honey and lemon, and she could stomach that.

In the Kingston of her childhood, she told me, every week her grandmother had chased her around the back of the house, brandishing a spoon and a bottle of cod liver oil. Her only escape then, she said, was up a tree, but her old grandma would still be there waiting for her, spoon in hand, when hunger drove her down.

So, honey and lemon she could stomach, but ten months on, she realised, she had a lot less voice than before. When she returned to the doctor, she said, he was obliged to admit that this ailment might merit a second opinion. She reckoned it was a full two weeks before she got to see the specialist who, without further discussion, sent her to have her throat X-rayed.

On the day of Fay's appointment, I sat with her in the radiography clinic. She was twitchy. Back in the dark ages, my grandparents' generation had put it about that people who went into hospitals rarely ever came back out. Our joint experiences with hospitals and family members seemed to corroborate this. I had taken my uncle – Fay's husband – to hospital not that many months before, and he hadn't come back out.

'You should ask for a receipt,' she said, 'before you deposit any of us at a hospital.'

Clustered in with the common herd, the two of us experienced a medical epiphany: we agreed that neither of us liked hospitals because they were full of sick people, and we reflected on the fact that in hospital waiting rooms, we were seeing only the workers, the pensioners, the unemployed. When I was rich, I told her, I wouldn't be seen dead anywhere near a National Health hospital. Never did I want to queue in these drab hellholes, I said, for fear of catching something from the person sitting next to me and where, surely, even the simple act of crossing the threshold or breathing the air could contaminate me. I would breathe, I told her, but I would not inhale. She agreed it was for the best.

A woman in a white overall walked into view, waving a set of X-rays in the air.

'Does anyone know,' she asked her colleagues in a booming voice, 'whose these are?'

That's how it worked in those days.

Fay turned to me, but before she could utter a suitable comment, she was called into the radiography room.

She emerged fifteen minutes later exactly as she had gone in, but with a chalky residue around her mouth.

'Horrible, horrible,' she said, scrubbing at her lips with the edge of a paper hankie.

'Which is why,' I told her, 'they sent us here. So the experience would be so bad that we'd never want to come back.' I was half-hoping the fright of being there would bring back her voice.

And time passed. A time of croakiness and whispers. Fay was summoned back to the hospital.

'Why?'

'I don't know. They didn't say.'

This time, I learned, they had put her into a deep sleep so they could slide a camera down her throat. She was in for two nights, cursing every minute of it. The women in her ward, she told me, were all in various stages of voicelessness. This, I gathered, was a circle of hell where each sinner received a punishment befitting the role they had played, or failed to play, in life. One of Fay's fellow patients was a teacher who, she told me, had shouted too long and too loudly at her pupils. Before her operation, she had gone from bed to bed telling the voiceless and the immobilised about her abscessed tonsils. Fay, as muted as the rest, could merely mouth imprecations. Only when the teacher's tonsils were removed, said Fay, was the woman adequately silenced.

I called the hospital to check when I could come and take my auntie home. She was waiting for her tablets, they told me, but just minutes later, as I turned into the hospital driveway in my car, I spotted her striding up the opposite side of the road in that feisty and assertive Caribbean way of hers. She'd just had a semi-voiceless argument with the nurses on the ward. She'd asked them when she could go home. She had been ready for the past four hours, she told them. A heated discussion ensued in which they told her she had to wait for her medication.

'What medication? I'm not on any medication,' she told them.

'Painkillers, then.'

She did not want any painkillers, she said. She was not in any pain. What she wanted to know was when she could go. She could go, they said… when she had got her medication. So enraged was she that she left herself speechless.

The doctors would have had us believe the growths on Fay's vocal cords were down to a lifetime of heavy smoking and drinking. I asked her if we must then assume she had been a very bad woman, and that the time had come for her to pay for her recklessness. This was likely, she said, since she was lined up for a six-week course of radiotherapy, for which she had gone back onto another waiting list. One thing was certain, and this we had agreed on. If she properly got her voice back, she would have plenty to say about it.

A new episode was about to begin in both our lives, though this I did not think wise to tell her at the time.

***

Wolf Haul

'Come in, my dear, come in.'

Cautious, tentative, hesitant, Blanche has entered; surprised by the sight in her granny's bedroom.

Her body stands straight; her eyes are holding the gaze, as if something might happen to change what she sees before her. Those ears, beneath the nightcap, flex in an uncommon fashion.

Blood at the corners of her granny's mouth – which glistens on yellowish teeth – slithers down the old woman's hairy neck in coagulating lumps. Blanche notes more. Her granny's eyes are huge; and if she stares, she can see herself reflected, and she can see that, distressingly, her red bonnet is askew.

'Come in, my dear, come in.' Her granny is growling at her, saliva dripping, hoping she will move even closer.

And at this point, depending on whether or not we like Blanche, we can change the ending if we want.

***

Photograph

The photographs propelled her back to another time, to different surroundings, and to emotions long forgotten. There was an energy in those memories. As Isabel came upon his image, she tensed. For what had previously been adoration was now anger and resentment.

In the snapshot, he was on horseback. That's how they had met – ridiculously, she thought now – on a horse safari, cavorting in his luxury tent, getting wasted on crates of the best Stellenbosch wines. He was pictured on a feisty young horse, sitting tall in the saddle, a hand on one hip, as if to say, 'Look at me! Look how confident I am, how special, how grand!'

And how idiotic, she thought. Of course, she had not thought this at the time. At the time, besotted, she had taken the photograph at his bidding. But she had been so much younger then. Well, perhaps not *that* young. She had, in any event, been caught up in the net of passion, and now she regretted it. In the long term, Pony Club had not benefited her.

With the point of her scissors, she ripped across his face, and down, and across, again and again until his image was entirely obliterated. And there were tears on her cheeks for all that she believed she had suffered, and all that she now repaid. She consigned the shreds of his photograph to the bin.

Just three days later, opening the newspaper at the page of obituaries, she found an extended account of his life. He had died unexpectedly just a few days earlier, a tragic accident, it said. She was stunned. She was also glad.

But that night she awoke anguished. It troubled her deeply this news about him. She thought of the power and effect of her actions – the cutting, the ripping, the slashing.

What she hoped and prayed for fervently was that nothing had happened to the horse.

***

Off the Mark

Billie was the seventh child of the seventh child, all of them girls. That should have counted for something. As far as she was concerned, it completed the enchantment requirements. And now she was about to put them to work. It was her boss she hated, the one who was the focus of her wrath, the one who was to be the subject of her incantation. She did not know if it would work, but she intended to try. She wasn't at all sure how this was done but she knew a person who did.

'Pour me another gin,' said Grandma. 'I need to think about this.'

Billie poured the gin.

'And have one yourself,' said Grandma. 'It'll do you good. Put a bit of colour in your cheeks. Help you think.'

'I don't like gin, Grandma,' said Billie.

'What's all this grandma this, grandma that?' said Grandma. 'I don't like it. Makes me feel ancient.'

'Well, what should I call you then?'

'You can call me… Finola,' said Grandma.

'Oh, all right,' said Billie, and she wrote the name down in her notebook. 'Now, Finola…'

'Yes?' said Grandma.

'What about this spell then?'

'Remind me,' said Grandma. 'Who is this person you're supposed to be cursing?'

'My boss,' said Billie. 'I'm not so much cursing her as killing her. She's horrible.'

'Mmm...' said Grandma, sipping her gin and licking her lips. 'You see, if you curse her, then she will suffer. But if you kill her, well... then you'll kill her. I mean, what satisfaction is there in that?'

Billie thought for a moment, staring up at the nicotine-coated ceiling. 'I hadn't thought of this as a satisfying kind of occupation, but now that you mention it, a curse might be better. Except that I suppose it might take a long time.'

'Yes, this is true,' said Grandma, 'but casting curses or simple spells are good for beginners, a sort of starter kit. You know what I mean?'

Billie crinkled her nose.

'You can't go into this lightly,' said Grandma. 'It's not easy, and things can go wrong.'

'I thought all I had to do was chant a few words and throw salt over my shoulder. Something like that.'

'You young people,' said Grandma, tapping her empty glass. 'All you want are quick fixes.'

'Well, yes,' said Billie. 'That would be nice. I can't wait ages and ages for something to happen to my boss. I want her gone now. She's an evil bitch and she is bringing misery upon us all... especially me.'

Grandma sat back, blinking. 'I see.' She struggled to her feet, leaning heavily on the table in front of her, and tottered the few feet to the teak bookcase that contained her weathered collection of instructional tomes. 'That one,' she said, 'pointing to a maroon-coloured leather volume. 'That one up there. Can you reach it?'

What Billie dropped heavily onto the tabletop was a recipe book of sorts. A creature ran out from under the cover as she flipped over the crinkly pages. 'You need a mothballs or something in here,' said Billie. 'Keep down the wildlife.'

'Now let's have a look at this,' said Grandma. 'Revenge, punishment, possession, bigamy…' She riffled through the leaves of the book at great speed. 'I don't want to give you anything too complicated to start with.'

'Right,' said Billie, 'and I'd prefer not to have to use dissected parts of reptiles and the like. I wouldn't know how to get all those bits and pieces anyway.'

'Mail order,' said Grandma. 'It's so much easier these days, and there are other methods you can apply. Internet, mobile phones…'

'Mmm…' said Billie. 'A simple enchantment will do, but can we do it now? I'd rather not wait.'

*

And so it was that returning to work the following day, Billie found her boss's office empty. She had written down the words. She had recited them in front of an open fire and then she had torn the words up and thrown the fragments of paper into the grate to be consumed by the flames. It gave her a kind of warm feeling, which was to be expected since she was sitting opposite hot coals. Today, as she exited the office, she noted that Sally, her boss's secretary was also not at her desk. She returned to her own office. On her computer there were no email messages advising staff of the demise of their leader. Billie was disappointed. She gazed out of the window and noted a white Mercedes in her boss's parking space. Who was that appropriating her boss's space, she wondered? Did it matter anyway? Her boss wouldn't be needing it. The car door opened, and out stepped… her boss.

*

'Grandma,' said Billie.

'Who?' said Grandma.

'Finola,' said Billie. 'That spell of yours. It didn't work.'

'Yes, well you're a beginner, dear. You can't really expect to get it right first time. Things can go wrong.' Grandma sighed, sipped at her drink, and chuckled to herself.

Billie gave her a fierce look.

'Just remembering my first time,' said Grandma. 'I'll tell you about it one day.'

'The secretary,' said Billie. 'You know, the one called Sally. She had a car accident. She's in one of those collars and she's going to be off work for three weeks.'

'Shame.'

'And my boss won a new car in a supermarket raffle. That wasn't supposed to happen, was it?'

'Oh, you know,' said Grandma, 'some you win, some you lose. You were a bit off the mark. That's all. Just mind when you cast the spells that no one else is in the vicinity.'

'What about poor Sally?' said Billie.

'Ah, yes,' said Grandma. 'Collateral damage.'

***

Hairdressing Tips

What with the hairdryers whirring and the *Musak* playing, Crystal couldn't seem to hear what Paul was saying to her.

'How do you know Deirdre?' he said.

'What?' said Crystal.

'Deirdre. How do you know her?'

'Oh, years,' she said, which was not exactly what he had asked.

He sent her packing to the washbasins. From time to time, he glanced over to see how she was getting on. Judging by the shampooist's expression, she was having the same problem with Crystal as he had.

Crystal was a referral, and Paul had been highly recommended. He hoped Deirdre had told Crystal that he was the best stylist in town. Then Crystal would tell her friends and her friends would tell other friends. You could never get enough recommendations, but it was tough pandering to the desires of women. And there were risks. What if you didn't meet up to a new client's expectations? You could be un-referred, and you could be un-recommended, and all because you put a parting on the wrong side of someone's head, or because you cut a woman's hair straight across at the nape, instead of fashioning it into a neat point.

When Crystal came back, turbaned, and ready for the scissors, Paul was set to pull out his repertoire of small talk.

'Sorry, I didn't catch that,' said Crystal. Her brow was furrowed.

Could it be that she was not happy? Paul was fast concluding that she was going to be very hard to impress.

Crystal looked up at his reflection in the mirror. Her eyes met his. 'I'm sorry,' she said, 'I've become very hard of hearing. Ever since the accident.'

'Accident?' said Paul.

And then she explained. She was a tad deaf, but she was far from dumb. She had lived in Naples, she told him. She was married there. One night she and her husband had been walking back from an evening out at a well-known restaurant when they had been caught in a bomb blast. Her husband's car had been targeted. She had been walking a few steps in front and had caught the full power of the blast. It had punctured her eardrums and she had suffered burns.

At this point in the conversation, Paul had already downed tools and, along with the shampooist, two assistants and another hairdresser, he was transfixed by this horrendous tale.

Crystal indicated her neck and upper chest. The skin was discoloured and strangely rippled. She was a woman with a history, a secret life that none of them could otherwise have imagined. If she had looked disgruntled, if she had seemed unhappy, well, it was hardly surprising given what she had been through.

Paul completed the job he had started. Crystal rose from her stylist's chair well contented, while around her there was an atmosphere of awe. She was a hero, a survivor of the violence of another land. At the reception desk, she took out her credit card to pay.

'No,' said Paul, sliding the card back across the counter, 'you're my guest. It's on the house.'

From the window, in silence, they all watched her climb into her car and drive away. She left without leaving a tip, but then who would expect a tip from someone who had endured so much?

Just a few days later, Deirdre arrived for her weekly wash and blow dry.

'Amazing woman, that Crystal,' said Paul, as Deirdre wriggled into place in front of the mirror.

'How's that?' said Deirdre.

And Paul, with as much detail as he could recall, related how he had learned of Crystal's terrible accident… the Neapolitan restaurant, the husband with the doubtful connections, the car bomb… and Crystal's irreversible and disfiguring injuries.

Deirdre listened unblinking and possibly – as it seemed to Paul – resigned, calm. Understanding?

'You see,' said Deirdre, 'it's like this. Crystal has never been married. There was no husband. She was never blasted by a bomb.'

Paul put down his comb and scissors, and stared back into the mirror at Deirdre. 'But,' he said.

'Yes?" said Deirdre.

'But the burns!' said Paul.

'Ah yes, the burns,' said Deirdre. 'When Crystal was seventeen, she lay too long by a Swiss lake in full summer, covered in baby oil. And got sunburn.'

'And her hearing!' said Paul.

'Well,' said Deirdre, 'I suppose there are some things in life that we want to hear, and other things we don't.'

***

The Necklace

'I hope you're satisfied,' said Storm, standing back to let her see the contents of the box.

Maxine took a deep breath. 'Yes,' she said. 'Yes, I am.' She stretched out her hand and touched the necklace with the tips of her fingers. 'Yes,' she whispered.

'Given what it cost us,' said Storm.

'It was worth it,' she said.

'A man's life?' He didn't wait for her answer. 'I don't understand you people.'

'Just take your money and go,' she said.

He took the envelope from the table, glanced inside, then stuffed it into his overcoat pocket. He looked at her for a moment, then strode towards the door, his coat flapping against the mahogany chairs as he wove his way through the salon of the *palazzo*. Before leaving, he turned. 'You know its history, of course,' he said. 'I'd take care if I were you.'

'I'll ask if I need your advice,' she said.

When she heard the outer door close behind him, Maxine stood for a long time admiring the piece. It glimmered in its box, its intricate filigree reflecting a golden light, the multifaceted stones catching the glow of the flickering table lamps. She could not count the years she had wished for the necklace. Now it was hers.

She held it up to the light. It was real. There was no doubt in her mind. This same necklace was the one worn by Lucrezia Borgia. It was the necklace gifted to Lucrezia by her brother. At its centre was the Star of Badshah Passand, the much-treasured stone that had once been set by an Indian craftsman into the browband of a horse's bridle... not the bridle of any horse, but that of a Sultan's prize stallion. Maxine knew the stories, that the gem had been removed from its rightful place and had assumed an existence of its own, taking on the life of those with whom it came into contact. It was a jewel that possessed not merely life, but the memory of life, and of death.

She stood in front of her bedroom mirror and held the necklace against her throat. Its touch was cool. She closed her eyes, her body swayed, and then it was as though her mind were filling with light.

She saw scenes she could never have imagined... of grandeur, of pomp, of armies assembled, of processions, of chests of gold, of tapestries and silken robes. She opened her eyes and carefully snapped the clasp into place at the nape of her neck. For these memories, she would have sacrificed the lives of thousands.

Her face glowed with the radiance of the necklace. It seemed to vibrate with a shimmering warmth, caressing her skin. She looked at it sideways on in the mirror. It was everything she had imagined. It held close to her neck, throbbing with its own life. She swallowed once, twice. She gasped. It had taken her breath away.

She looked again in the mirror. The necklace had risen higher around her throat. It no longer draped itself at her neck but seemed to have climbed against her flesh. And it tightened. She grasped it, digging her nails between it and her throat. But, even as she wrenched at it, it tore itself from her grip. And then it shrank, tighter and tighter until the blood ran and when, coughing, spluttering, gagging for air, she looked at her image for the last time in the mirror, she saw not her face but that of some other woman from ages past, a memory come to life… and death.

***

House

She was afraid to leave the room that overlooked the garden, the room with the wind-up gramophone. The corridor that led to the hallway and drawing room was always in darkness. To enter it was like walking into a blackened ball of cotton wool, muffled and musty, void of air.

This was how Helena remembered it, and she would see herself stepping into that darkness, her eyes intent on the light beyond, as if this would keep her safe from what waited. And just halfway from salvation it would happen, as she had known it would. He would lunge at her, giving out a deep guttural growl that merged with her screams, and his hands would dangle above her, his long tendril fingers waving like vines in her face so that she thought her heart would split from the terror of it. And sometimes his face was masked, and sometimes she felt his cloak sweep over and envelop her, and then she would feel his hands grip her and she would be hoisted high into the air, the sensation of being in a fast-moving lift where your stomach is left behind as the rest of you departs upwards. And at this point, her eyes would be squeezed shut, and the hiss in her ears, the fossilized scream of always, would become music, warm, and smooth.

Eyes open now, above her she would see the ceiling spin within a cascade of light and, before her, the face of her uncle, his own eyes half-closed as he swayed her to the rhythm of the music. And so, they danced, twirling, bowing, her short legs dangling above the carpet, above the furniture. Now she saw the fireplace, now the sideboard, now the huge oak table where her grandmother would sit to write, the sofa, the armchairs, the family photos on the walls, the image of the uncle who had died in the war, the holy statues of those who would protect the living. And then, her father standing by the door, frowning, angry, wordless, but at the next spin, gone. From the kitchen she would hear raised voices. Only then would her uncle lower her to the ground, after which she would laugh and beg for the haunting to begin again.

When the two men met on the stairs, unsmiling they nodded and passed on. Helena saw it but did not understand. They shared the house. Her home was upstairs with her father and mother, her grandmother and uncle downstairs. Her uncle downstairs with his girlfriends, his 'women.' Thinking back, she could remember one or two of them, but she remembered that she had loved them all. At the time, when she was at school, she hadn't grasped it. Her uncle talked of them freely to her. What would her father have said if he had known?

There was the ugly girlfriend, and the one too old for him. There was the one whose family paid him off. After all, what would a young woman's family want with a man who went out each day selling refrigerators? There was the one he couldn't see in the dark, only the whites of her eyes. Helena demanded to hear his story over and over, how he had seen her in the street, proud, haughty, magnificent, and had followed her more than once.

'Come and have dinner with me,' he had begged but, unimpressed, she had tossed her head and walked on. He knew that she was the one. She refused him until she too knew that *he* was the one.

Even with the conflict marring their cohabitation, Helena's father told her mother that they should buy the house – the house that they rented – and her mother told Helena's grandmother that he was thinking of buying the house. But her grandmother said that they would be fools and that the house would be nothing but a millstone around their necks. They could never afford it. Never. He earned five pounds, fifteen shillings a week. Just that to support the three of them, and pay their share of the rent. There was little to put aside. The house would cost them a thousand pounds. Where would they get money like that? No one in their family would ever have that kind of money. Helena told her mother that she would save up and give them the money.

'Yes, you will,' said her mother. 'I know you will, but these things take time. We'll have to be patient and wait for you, until you become rich and important.'

Helena never knew why they left the house. She sensed that cycle of existence was drawing to a close. She would see her grandmother sleeping, hardly moving, hardly breathing, and she imagined that the woman's death would be like this. And, whenever the house was silent, she imagined that it would be like that when all of them were gone. The clock ticking. The sound of emptiness.

Whatever happened, life changed and then life became death, then life again. Perhaps the lease expired and could not be renewed. Her recollections awoke in a different time and place, and with them came a sense of missingness.

Her memories lived on only in the photographs on the walls of her New York apartment, the house, the garden, her parents' wedding, she and her cousins sitting on the front steps. Helena's apartment was not her home, nor would it ever be. She told her Board of Directors that she was going home, that she would work out of the London office. It was her company, her business. She could do as she pleased, move from city to city, restless, without roots.

She returned many times to stare at the house. Next to the front gate, a 'For Sale' sign rattled in an autumn wind. From the outside, the building appeared unchanged, but the windows were unblinking and unlit at night, and the garden, or what she could see of it, was unkempt like uncombed hair. A bush of white roses scrambled recklessly above the walls. She had had a cat that died, and they had buried it in the garden. Her father dug the hole. Her mother planted the roses. Her grandmother said it wasn't allowed and her mother said that it hardly mattered since only they would ever know.

When the estate agent showed her the house prospectus, she did not flinch when he indicated the asking price. She could, of course, make an offer, he told her. She did not wish to bargain with her past. Nor did she have to. Not now. She knew her father would be glad for it not to be a millstone around her neck. She wanted back what had been taken from her. She would have it for her father and for her mother. She wanted for the millstone to be lifted from her grandmother's neck, for her uncle to forever play his gramophone. She could give them now what it had not been in her power to give before.

Perhaps the agent was mildly surprised that Helena did not need to tour the interior of the building. It was true that many people bought unseen, possibly to sell on. But no, she said, she would be living there herself. What she wanted was to enter that corridor again and to hear the music of the house. Their house.

As she signed the papers, the agent interrupted her.

'I feel I should tell you,' he said, and he laughed, 'we've had a few clients who said they were sure the house was haunted.'

'Oh yes,' she said, 'so I've heard.'

***

Visibility

You may have noted that, at some point in her life, every woman will drive into a storm. The day Gemma crashed her car, there was very bad visibility. It happened from time to time that there would be thoughtless storms like this whenever, in that distant but highly proactive land, they seeded the clouds. The visibility was far worse from Gemma's viewpoint as she refused to slide down her windows and look out. This was because she had just come from the hairdresser, and the rain and the wind and the sand would have spoiled her hair. So, she drove into that fog of rain, wind, and sand. She could not see through her windscreen. And she crashed her car into the black and yellow striped border of a very large roundabout.

'We'll have to get you to do an eye test,' said the policeman who was called to the scene.

'Oh, but it was nothing to do with my eyes,' said Gemma. 'It was my hair.'

***

A Visit to the Museum

Incident One. Engineer Hussain, on an assignment to repair Louise's A/Cs, stepped into a first-floor bathroom and then, in all haste, stepped back out again.

'Sorry, sorry, sorry,' he said.

He had seen something that he would remember with shame for the rest of his life: a woman, albeit crucially hidden in a voluminous skirt, sitting on the toilet with her knickers down around her ankles.

'Sorry, sorry, sorry,' he said as he left the house never to return.

The woman, hardly fazed, was Jessica, temporary house guest of Louise, who was in turn the friend of Christine, who had brought Jessica with her to Abu Dhabi from Riyadh, where they both worked.

'Whatever were you thinking of?' said Christine. 'Why didn't you lock the door?'

After the incident, Jessica had repaired to the kitchen, where she had mixed an abundant margarita with a judicious application of crushed ice. Reposing now in an armchair in Louise's lounge, she was unapologetic.

'I didn't know someone was going to walk into the bathroom. I just never lock bathroom doors.'

Christine gave Louise a knowing look, but Louise did not know what the knowing in the look was meant to mean. Jessica was a third party, brought along by Christine for reasons unknown – to keep her company? – and she was possibly, or so Louise thought, a liability, judging by her initial rather dubious behavior.

Incident Two. Jessica sidled into Louise's room, a tequila refill in hand and wearing just her balconette uplift bra and a wrap-over skirt in an ethnic print. Lounging on Louise's bed, uninvited, she advised her about the benefits of Botox. Louise was not amused. In fact, she was ever so slightly offended.

'Look,' said Jessica. 'I've had it here and here and here,' and with that she prodded at her eyes and brows, letting her drink dribble out of her glass onto Louise's duvet.

Incident Three. When the taxi came to take the three of them to the restaurant where they were to celebrate Christine's birthday, Jessica immediately flung herself into the seat next to Kamil the driver from Peshawar. Both Christine and Louise gestured to her to squeeze into the back seat with them, but she was having none of it.

'And where are *you* from?' she said, squeezing the arm of the bemused driver.

She indulged in much stretching and yawning throughout the trip, creating some degree of distraction both for the driver himself and those who came to a halt next to their car at traffic lights.

At the close of that particular evening, Christine had a number of comments to make to Jessica about the propriety of her behavior, or lack of it, about the avoidance of lewd mannerisms and idle talk. Back at the villa, slumped cozily in an armchair with a nightcap of rum and Coke by her side, Jessica listened without comment.

'So, do you see what I'm getting at here, Jessica?' said Christine.

And Jessica replied with the soft clucking of the contentedly comatose.

Incident Four. After a busy shopping expedition in the mall, Jessica and Christine enjoyed a lavish lunch with aperitifs and a bottle of wine. In the bathroom, Jessica was disturbed by the sudden appearance of a figure at the entrance to her cubicle, a man in a business suit.

'Oh, my goodness!' said the man. 'I do apologize.'

Jessica emerged unflustered, adjusting her undergarments, and told the man that it was all right and that he needn't worry.

'Well, no,' he stammered, 'but then, it *is* the men's bathroom, after all.'

Was it not strange, observed Christine, that there had been two bathroom incidents in the space of two days? Whatever was it – yet again – that Jessica was thinking of?

Louise endured it all stoically. After all, Jessica was Christine's friend, she reminded herself, not hers. While she felt obliged to monitor the situation in case she fell foul of Jessica's misdemeanors, she believed the bulk of the responsibility lay with Christine, whose duty it was to chaperone her companion and keep her out of harm's way. In this respect, Louise was confident that whatever disrespectful *faux pas* Jessica might commit, she – Louise – need never be held responsible. This reassuring state of affairs was destined to collapse, however.

Due to an airline scheduling glitch, Christine and her friend were booked on separate flights out of Abu Dhabi. Christine's return flight to Riyadh was on a Thursday morning, while Jessica's was on the afternoon of the following day. Louise experienced an unpleasant flush of heat throughout her body as she came to understand the significance of these departure times. Her sole house guest, from Thursday through to Friday, would be Jessica, the very person with whom she would never have chosen to spend her leisure time.

Christine reassured her friend that it was only a matter of a few hours, and it was not as if Jessica were an unfeeling and inconsiderate monster. She did, after all, live in a country that was far more restricting and taboo-observant than the rest of the entire Gulf put together, and she had done so for nearly eight years without significant incident. Sometimes, Christine pointed out, we expect the worst, we agonize over potential pitfalls, we effectively torment ourselves, and nothing happens. It is often the case, she said, that we attach far too much importance to tiny unimportant events and explode them into vast diplomatic incidents when in reality they have little or no impact except for the weight with which we ourselves endow them.

Louise had never taken kindly to what she perceived as scolding or lecturing. To her, Christine appeared so attached to this misfit that she was living in denial of her faults. As she saw it, Christine was Jessica's keeper. She herself was not. And now it was as if Christine were cruelly abandoning her and leaving her burdened with a headstrong and irresponsible child.

'What you must do, Christine,' she said, 'is make it clear to Jessica that she has to mind her p's and q's.' Louise was perhaps preaching to the converted when she told Christine that *she* was the one who had to live there, and if Jessica were to offend the highly conservative residents of this otherwise liberal city, it was Louise herself who would suffer the consequences – all because of an unwished-for houseguest, though she did not speak this last thought so as not to alienate her friend. Nor did she mention to Christine that just that day her next-door neighbor Huda had invited the three of them over to visit. Louise had accepted the invitation before learning that Christine was about to depart and now, in a tormented interior monologue, she was imagining how she might proffer an excuse to her neighbor. She considered her two options. The first was to disentangle herself from the invitation and risk the displeasure of her neighbor, who might perceive her withdrawal as a snub – and locals did not like to be snubbed. The second option was to maintain good relations with Huda and do the house visit with Jessica in tow and on best behavior. But, if Christine, Jessica's loyal and loving friend, could not guarantee her best behavior, what hope had *she*?

Incident Five. Incident Five hadn't yet happened, but Louise thought it might… soon.

When she returned from delivering Christine to the airport, she entered an unusually silent house. Alarmed at first, she was pleased to find Jessica watching daytime TV in the lounge with the volume turned low. Following instructions, Jessica had lunched alone and was now sitting quietly watching *Homeland* on Netflix. On closer inspection, her eyelids drooped, and her face radiated a warm glow. Louise suspected the worst, and sure enough, she found three empty beer bottles deposited in the garbage bin, and three substitutes – not yet cold – replacing them on the top shelf of the fridge.

'We're supposed to be going to the neighbors,' wailed Louise. 'They're going to smell the beer on your breath.'

'They'll never notice,' said Jessica. 'And, I don't intend getting that close.'

'You could have waited till we got back.'

'I'm on holiday,' she said.

Huda was alone except for the three maids – two Indonesian, one Sudanese – and miscellaneous small children. Her husband Abdullah, she told them, had given up his weekend at home to attend a conference on leadership skills at a seven-star hotel in Dubai. Left to devise her own amusement, Huda welcomed this excuse to give her visitors a tour of house and garden.

Now that the evenings were beginning to cool, she had purchased new outdoor furniture from Ace Hardware, along with a miniature bouncy castle for the children, which could be viewed comfortably from the windows of the lounge. She had relandscaped the garden, courtesy of Mr. Asif of Bangla Panoramas, though, as she pointed out, he acted only on her instructions and brought little of his own imagination to the task. In addition to the pink-and-white-flowering bougainvillea, she had banana and mango trees, an array of multicolored peonies, and an ample vegetable patch. She could not describe to them, she said, the intense happiness she experienced when cooking meals – with the assistance of her three maids – using produce fresh from her very own garden.

As to other provisions, and in advance of the Eid celebrations, she was sure that Louise must have noticed in the empty plot behind her house, the four young goats she had recently bought from a farmer in Sweihan.

Louise remarked that she had indeed seen one of the maids climbing over the boundary wall each morning to feed and water these fine animals. As they spoke, Huda plucked a selection of herbs from the beds that were located on either side of the newly built guest annex. Members of her husband's family often visited from Al Ain, she said, and now in this small building, which comprised a modern bathroom and bedroom, both furnished with attractive accessories from Home Centre and The One, they could enjoy a modicum of privacy away from the main house.

From time to time, Louise did a visual check of Jessica to reassure herself that all was well. Apart from the brief sneezing fit induced by the obligatory sniffing of the herbs, everything seemed normal. Once seated in the main lounge, a family *majlis* of sorts, the maids served the three women with tall glasses of lemon and mint, each decorated with a tiny cardboard parasol, stamped all over with minute images of the national flag.

This was an original idea Huda had had while on holiday in Mauritius. On her return, she had bought the parasols in bulk, online from a Chinese supplier.

At this point Huda left the room to fetch the parasol brochure and, in her absence, Jessica indicated to Louise that she needed a bathroom since her beers had now come full circle.

'I think you should wait,' said Louise.

'No,' said Jessica, 'I would like to use a bathroom now.'

Huda, brochure in hand, caught this last statement on re-entry. She directed her guest to the bathroom in the new annex, and Jessica, perspiring slightly, set off at great speed out of the front door, past the potted aloe vera and bougainvillea, and down the marble steps of the villa. She was gone some time.

When she came back, Louise, who now knew everything there was to know about customizing her parasols, gave her a questioning look. Jessica returned a gracious and enigmatic smile.

Her behavior throughout was exquisite. She discussed food: the merits of Big Macs versus Shake Shack burgers. She applauded Huda's clothing, the *abayas* made for her to her own designs by Mr. Mohammed Tarik of the Pink Orchid Tailoring Agency. She admired the delightful, curly-headed children who, as the women spoke, crawled under and over the sofas. She complimented Huda on her superb choice of furnishings, handpicked from the Golden Furniture store on Airport Road. Jessica and Louise might well have remained, but for the fact that Huda received a call on her iPhone and became absorbed in a conversation with a friend, leaving her guests to watch the cartoons on TV with the toddlers. Fifteen minutes later, Louise and Jessica tiptoed out, blowing kisses to their hostess.

At home, it was Louise herself who took care to prepare the drinks, the tiniest measure of vodka for Jessica with extra ice cubes, and something with a little more punch for herself. She thought of it as a reward for the travails of that culturally charged visit. The time was right, she felt, to take it upon herself to explore with Jessica the reasons for her misdemeanors.

'So, this bathroom thing,' said Louise. 'What's that all about?'

Jessica stared into her drink and did not speak. She looked a broken woman. Louise had touched a nerve, it seemed, but it at last prompted a confession. It was, said Jessica, all down to a visit she had once made to a museum: the world-renowned Hermitage in Saint Petersburg. Everything came back to that one fateful day.

Incident Pre-Incident. For years, Jessica told Louise, she had dreamed of going on a visit to the museum. She had Russian blood – royal ancestral blood – on her mother's side and, though she never spoke of it, she could feel her roots pulling her back to the land of her origins. When that day arrived and she found herself on a holiday package in Saint Petersburg, in that sacred place, her joy was without bounds. So often in life, she said, we reach false conclusions about people based merely on their speech and appearance. Possibly, looking at her, Louise could never have imagined the desire that she carried in her heart to be one with such magnificence, such beauty.

As the guide ushered the tourists, a group of fellow Americans, from room to room, Jessica could not help but linger as long as she could amongst these glories of the past. But nature called and, in her search for a bathroom, she found herself, she said, in a small anteroom that contained a variety of artifacts, oriental vases large and small. But what held her was the portrait of a woman, a familiar face, looking down on her with a loving expression in her deep sapphire eyes. So absorbed was Jessica that she did not hear the sound of a door shutting and the click of a key turning in a lock.

She called. She screamed. She hammered. There was no signal on her phone. Hours passed. It grew dark. The walls closed in on her. The portrait ceased to smile. When she was finally released by a patrolling security guard, she was greatly changed.

On hearing this, Louise was filled with remorse. Knowing now what Jessica had been through and how it had damaged her, she berated herself for having been so hard on her.

'That's a terrible story, Jessica,' she said. 'Thank you for sharing it with me.'

Jessica smoothed a tear from her cheek and the two women sat for some moments without speaking.

'I think,' said Louise, 'that you were just unlucky with those two bathroom incidents. Thank goodness nothing went wrong when we went to Huda's. I have to admit I started to worry when you were gone such a long time.'

'Yes,' said Jessica. 'That would be because I was looking for a bathroom. The one she sent me to was locked. So, I had to go elsewhere.' She fished a lump of ice from her glass and popped it into her mouth. Louise could hear her crunch it between her back teeth.

'You were a bit mean with the vodka, Louise,' said Jessica.

En route to the airport the following day, Jessica commented that she had never liked flying and it was a miracle she managed to get on any plane.

'Well,' said Louise, 'You got here so – *insha'allah* – you should be able to get back. Do you need the bathroom?'

'No,' said Jessica.

As soon as she reached home, Louise snatched the one remaining beer from the fridge. She threw herself onto the sofa, closed her eyes and drank, enjoying the sting of the icy liquid on her tongue. She congratulated herself on a job well done. When she called Christine's number to let her know the merchandise was on its way and, more importantly, to reveal to her that she now knew what was going on with Jessica, far from exhibiting surprise, Christine asked Louise outright if Jessica had told her about 'that awful business in Saint Petersburg.'

That Christine was already aware of this incident, and had evidently known about it for some time, shocked Louise. If she had only known at the outset that Jessica was in the throes of some kind of post-traumatic stress, things might have been so much simpler, or at least she might have behaved more compassionately towards Jessica. Why, she asked, had Christine not explained all this to her?

At the other end of the line, Christine gave a sigh.

'Louise,' she said, 'I have to tell you something. You see, before Jessica came to Riyadh, she had never been out of Wisconsin. I mean, she's never been to Russia. Ever. Never been to Saint Petersburg. It's nothing to do with small rooms, or locked doors, or claustrophobia, or being damaged.'

'Oh!' said Louise.

'Most likely,' continued Christine, 'it's to do with the joys of liberty, of overindulgence. In short… of alcohol. By the way, have you counted the beers in your fridge? Also, I wonder.' She paused. 'Have you heard from Huda yet? And, I'm assuming,' she said in conclusion, 'that you made sure Jessica used the bathroom before she got on the plane.'

Incident Six…

***

Good Girl

In 1966, Veronica won the Form 1 Prize for Good Conduct. She received a navy-blue hessian sash and a tiny enamel badge with the letter 'C' on it. For her lack of sins, when she ran about the playground, her Good Conduct sash would slip from her shoulder and trip her up at the ankles.

The following year, Veronica won the Form 2 Prize for Good Conduct: a powder blue hessian sash, and the same enamel badge presented again.

The year after that, Veronica's house mistress announced that, since it had been noted that Veronica was naturally quiet and well-behaved, she would no longer be awarded the Good Conduct Prize. She had, after all, made no effort to win it in the previous two years.

Now in her mid-sixties, Veronica is thankful for the day she lost the prize, was unfettered, and was given licence to be bad.

***

Evelyn's Virtual Diary

Oneday

Forsday is my origination day. I had almost forgotten. I strolled into the lounge with my bowl of Coco Pops (penultimate packet) and the entire AnimaDisk lit up. 'Good morning, Evelyn,' it said. 'This is to advise you that your expiry approaches. Please select your date and time of processing.'

I need to think this through.

Twosday

When I go, I may take a few with me. What do I care? Frank will be top of my list. He dropped by yesterday morning with a large tube of decorative vitamites, and he saw the message. He said he hadn't realised I was *that* old. I really didn't look it and it was amazing what they could do these days.

He asked if I was going to throw a deletion party.

Threesday

I stepped out to gather a few vegetables from my patch – real food – and before I knew it, I had a gaggle of bloated little plastikids around me, tubby little stomachs, fat legs and double chins. I may be old, but I can still walk and run, which is more than I can say for them.

Are they old enough to drive those SlipShoes?

Forsday

A circle of fluorescent flowers lit up the AnimaDisk this morning. The message read,

On this origination day,

With joyous voice we say

'Happy Hundreth, Evelyn!'

I nearly puked. Underneath, it said,

Congratulations! Your processing is booked at Yoothanazium for 12 noon on Fivesday.

We hope you had a good life and we wish you a smooth departure.

Finding the tube empty, Frank said it wasn't a good idea to down so many vitamites in one go. Colourful they may be, but they are not sweeties. Too true. They are, however, tempting to plastikids with fast shoes.

Fivesday

[Click here to enter your thoughts.]

HISTORICAL NOTES ON EVELYN'S VIRTUAL DIARY

"The desires of today are the errors of our tomorrow."

Evelyn Coomber, 2061

Evelyn transferred her kreditz into powndz on the BlakMarkit. This enabled her to live out the rest of her days comfortably in Bermooda.

We understand that Evelyn reached the Bakovbeeyond under her own steam as it were, wearing a pair of SlipShooz, which she obtained from a plastikid through the barter of a large quantity of multicoloured vitamites.

The government's 'Perfekt Children for All' manifesto was rejected but the idea appealed to, and was supported by, the affluent middle klasses who subsequently reverted to the services of popular providers such as Optimal Offspring and ChildPerfekt.

Plastikids were intended as first-generation origination improvements. Their facial features were to be corrected and recalibrated at intervals of between one to five years. Teeth could be straightened at origination, while skin and feature defects could be controlled through painless sinthetik injections.

Plastikids were eventually discontinued. Initially, the government's 'No sport at skool' policy, which had been designed with the aim of protecting plastikids from injury, had the effect of nurturing obesity. Later, due to a preponderance of law soots against teachers, home skooling through Interactive AnimaViz replaced regular skooling. However, long-term AnimaViz exposure resulted in a number of horrific meltdown incidents in plastikid subjects that had been treated with advanced sinthetiks.

It would seem that Evelyn used a RetroPC for the writing of her diary. There is no trace of this hardware but, miraculously, paypa hardcopy of her document survived and is now preserved in the Heritage Moozeyum.

Evelyn's work came to light through research undertaken by the Society for the Preservation of Ritten Rekordz. The Society seeks to conserve our linguistic heritage and supports the reinstatement of ritten documentation, the skill of riting and an appreciation of "classical" speling. The Society advocates the standardisation of speling. (Note Ben: A number of critics have denounced the inconsistency of the Society's own ritten output and akordingly efforts are being made to remedy this.)

The decline of the ritten word began with the rise in popularity of text messages, which we at the Society believe handicapped and de-skilled our young people. Around 2040, works of fiction submitted for the Booker Prize were limited to a maximum of 50,000 words per book. Publishers eventually applied this rule to all books, mainly for financial reasons. But the fact was that, increasingly, the general public was finding it a strain to read 'long books' on their book devices. It was only a question of time before official riting was limited to 250 words per communication (though this could be interpreted liberally).

Research revealed that the excessive use of sinthetikz was in fact affecting brain-eye coordination with the result that attention spans were declining steadily. University dissertations were rarely longer than 1,000 words. However, most educated people could not read more than 250 words at one sitting. The 'man in the street' could not manage even 250 words in a month... hence the return of oralkulture. It is highly probable that if you are able to read thus far, you will be a second generation klonak.

The practice of having oneself cloned and thus drawing on previously learned and arkival knowledge is common in the field of akademia. Certainly it does give akademics the edge both where their students and their unkloned colleagues are concerned. The only disadvantage with this procedure is that the subject must be deceased in order to undergo processing.

Evelyn's neighbour and would-be suitor Frank was deleted by appointment at Yoothanazium in 2082.

Evelyn herself died peacefully in her sleep at the age of 152. A statue was erected in her honour in the grand foyer of the Heritage Moozeyum but, following requests from the public, this was later replaced by a plak engraved as follows:

Evelyn Coomber 1951-2103

A life prolonged is experience gained

In recognition of Evelyn's heroic flight from deletion, the statue itself was transferred to the Moozeyum's gardens so that Evelyn's free spirit could gaze across the vast yellow plains of Bakovbeeyond.

***

Preparedness

If Sandra had not prepared for the storm, the consequences would have been disastrous... deckchairs blown into nearby fields, tiles swept from the porch roof, garden furniture splintered into pieces of wood ready for the next bonfire, plant pots smashed, flowers butchered. Her life disrupted. A loss of order.

So, she *did* prepare for the storm, folding the deckchairs, securing tiles, shifting and stacking garden furniture, putting pots and flowers in places of safety.

But, since the storm never came, she moved everything back. Though for the life of her, where it all originally went, she could scarce remember.

***

Furniture

She had never liked other people's furniture. It wasn't their taste that concerned her, whether she liked what they chose or not. It was the spirit they infused within the furniture.

The way Gail saw it, every chair, every table, every bed – particularly every bed – had a life, had lived a life, and was a fount of thought and memory. She was not sure that she could live with the memories of others.

When Marcus said he needed to move away to write, she was disturbed.

'Away where?' she said.

'You know,' he said. 'A cottage somewhere. Maybe by the sea or by a lake, somewhere I can see out across a landscape.'

'You've got a landscape here. Why can't you write here?'

'It's not a landscape,' said Marcus. 'It's a garden.'

He saw this, she realised, as a question of location, while for her it was a question of the familiar versus the unfamiliar, the personal versus the impersonal. In her own home, the touch of her surroundings radiated through her body and gave her a sense of reassurance. She was safe among the memories she had created or inherited: her grandmother's sideboard, her parents' bed, the wardrobe she had had built by a local carpenter. As Gail moved about her home, she noted the slight shifts in the location of her furniture. She knew if her furniture was happy or sad. Sometimes she would be happy, but her furniture was sad. The furniture had a mind of its own.

When Marcus had moved into the shed at the bottom of the garden, she thought it strange but she accepted the strangeness, and so did her furniture. He was, after all, a writer and was allowed to diverge from the norm. But, clearly, he did not feel the mood of his immediate surroundings in the way that she did. His thoughts were taken up with the book that was due, the advance that had been paid, and the editor who would visit to 'monitor' his progress. He could, and should, be forgiven.

Viewing his behaviour from a distance, Gail would describe it to herself. And she imagined what her furniture would say about Marcus's rejection of it. She committed these thoughts to paper, in an elegant hand, and using the ancient ballpoint that was once her father's.

As Marcus sat in his shed, studying the daffodils, Gail sat in her kitchen listening to the words of her own characters, their anger, their sadness, their resentment. Why would Marcus want to distance himself? Were they, the table, the chairs, the cupboards not inspiration enough? And now he longed for the country and the furniture of others. The mood of the furniture turned from dismay to envy, envy of the unknown furniture of another home that was luring Marcus away. This, too, she wrote about as Marcus, in his limbo of the garden shed, wrote nothing at all.

With suitable reverence, Gail prepared a tray of tea and biscuits for the visitor – her mother's teapot, the cups and saucers she had bought for one of her parents' anniversaries, a tablecloth given to her by an aunt. The editor, phone in hand and wearied from an undesired but necessary journey across town, collapsed into her father's favourite chair, and sat on the cushion sewn by her grandmother.

'I'll go and fetch Marcus,' said Gail. 'Try the biscuits. I made them myself.' And with that, she set off down the garden path to alert Marcus to pause his writing and come up to the house. She found him texting, his screensaver scrolling motivational messages across his laptop.

'All right?' she said.

'Yeah,' said Marcus.

'Jill's here.'

'Okay,' he said, and sighed. 'Be up in a minute.'

Re-entering the kitchen, Gail found Jill leaning up against the sink, reading from the notebook she had left on the table.

Jill looked up. Alert now, her eyes sparkled. 'So, what's this?' she said.

***

Hotel

The hotel was deserted this time of year. The woman viewed the dark clouds from a window overlooking the abandoned pool. She thought she should go out, but the weather was foul. Every time one of the hotel staff stepped out through the swing doors, a howl of icy wind blew in a wave of wizened leaves. She chose to stay inside, and inside there was precious little but employees to-ing and fro-ing and the occasional guest, a businessman perhaps, a young couple passing through.

She rode the lift up and down, always seeming to have forgotten something. Was it here on this floor? Or was it on the next? She sometimes confused one floor for another. She observed the peculiarities of different floors. Here was the floor with the coffee-stained carpet. Here was the floor with the silver-grey waste bin. Here the floor with the door marked 'private.' From time to time, she would see the cleaners huddled in a stairwell, talking in a language she could not understand. Arriving at the same floor on different occasions, she would find objects added and then removed, a scarf draped over an armchair would disappear when she returned the next time around. On an empty table in a lobby, she would find a book when she came that way again.

Sometimes the lights were on and sometimes they were off. She passed silently from one space to the next, from one lobby to another. The clocks, she noted, showed different times. She would see the shadows of people moving behind opaque glass doors, but she met no one, she spoke to no one. She heard the lift rise and fall and she would hear voices and have a sense of invisible activity about her.

Much later, or what seemed to her like much later, she took a seat in one of the various atriums. People passed her by. She looked up to catch their eye, to pass the time of day, but no one looked in her direction except once for a child who stood before her and stared unsmiling and insolent. She stared back. She had no children of her own. Why should she have any interest in other people's? The child's parents called him. He turned and left.

She found herself forgetful. She would forget a glove, a notebook, a pencil. She would put them down and then miss them. Shortly after she would see those objects again and wonder who had left them there. Then she remembered that *she* must have, but she could not remember when.

In the lift, she met a woman of about her age. She asked herself why this woman would choose to be here. She thought the woman could be on holiday or on business or, perhaps, meeting someone. She watched as the woman looked at herself in the lift mirror, arranged her hair, removed a smudge of make-up from below her eye. Then the woman sighed and exited the lift.

This may have happened recently or a long time ago. She was not sure. She thought then that she would check her emails. But maybe she had already done this. In any event, she found the other woman at the computer, checking her emails. She slipped away and let the woman continue without speaking to her. She thought of going to lunch but she was not hungry. And thinking about eating or not eating, she had a sense that she had been here before, but she could not remember and had no evidence of having been here. She looked in her journal, flicked through the pages and saw that the last entry was dated a year before. She was staying in a hotel not unlike this one, in the same room, wearing the same clothes. Something of this she recalled.

After so much rain, a blade of sun was out. She could feel the warmth on her face. Below her stretched the town, white-walled, red-roofed, and beyond, the houses, the sand, the surf, the sea, its blue turned grey, and a fogged horizon reaching to cloud. She could remember – was remembering – old acquaintances. She saw their faces. She heard their voices. They spoke her name, gave advice, made comments, laughed even.

In the restaurant, she sat in her preferred place, a table opposite the plate glass windows through which she saw the beach. A single waitress moved around her, coming and going, bringing food and collecting empty plates. She could not remember now if she had eaten or was about to eat. She had no sensation of hunger. In the window she saw her own reflection. It occurred to her that there came a moment when we were face-to-face with our own mortality. She was not sure what she understood by that, but she knew this thought held meaning for her in some dimension of her being. But, what being was that, she wondered? And when she looked up to enquire of her reflection in the glass, her reflection was no more. In its place, she saw an empty fading chair.

She might return here, she thought, or perhaps she already had.

***

LEAVING

When they gave Rachel the letter, they said she could leave right away if she wanted to, provided she'd finished the clearance procedures. She'd need to hand in her office keys, take back her library books, give up her gate pass. Khalid would cancel her visa. The accommodation was all paid up so, for now at least, she could stay. But then there was the issue of the utilities, the bank account, the phone, the health insurance. There was the business of rehoming or exporting the animals. Without the visa, all would be withdrawn or made invalid.

Fatima said Rachel could pay for a temporary visa, or perhaps find another job. 'Or, you could just go.'

Two and a half months later, still into the packing, had she been in that other place – the place where she was going – she would not have survived. What Elvira had done, she would have done too.

*

They came back from the beach that day, Anja and her husband, and saw the sky turn grey and the air become mist.

'We passed your area,' Anja told Rachel afterwards, 'but then the fire seemed distant.'

The fire is always distant until you look again.

After eating they were tired and turned in for the night, but Anja slept poorly. She woke at three and went outside. There was an orange glow on the horizon.

*

In her thoughts, Rachel often replayed her meeting with Elvira. Maybe it was something she did to express her thanks. That she could not speak the woman's language did not concern her. Elvira had come that day to welcome her. Rachel explained what she could about herself, her name, and where she was from. Elvira took her by the arm and led her to a shaded spot at the foot of a sloping meadow behind Rachel's newly purchased house.

'There,' she said, pointing upwards, while a small dog yapped and scurried at their feet. 'That's where we live,' she said. 'The house with the brown-wood awning.'

Rachel could not identify it at first. Then, shading her eyes, she saw Elvira's house. It overlooked the landscape, and she and Elvira were in the landscape, in its view.

*

Rachel was not ready. She wasn't ready to lose her job. She wasn't ready to move. Sometimes not being ready in life is a good thing, better than not being ready in death.

In the desert, she would ride her horse along one of many tracks. They were all either long or short, but they went in different directions beneath the descending sun, across sand, gravel, shrub. She told herself that the short tracks were safer because she was less likely to find herself under the Sheikh's helicopter, or spooked by another horse, or surprised by a herd of gazelle. But it is not the length of time or distance that matters. What is going to happen will happen, even in the blink of an eye. You need to accept it and try to be ready when it comes.

*

There's a place for each of us somewhere, Rachel believed, to merge, connect, be accepted, start again. Elvira told her she was welcome and she must come and visit. Months earlier, it was what Rachel had hoped for when, sensing an ending, she had bought her house. This stranger hugged her, kissed her on both cheeks, and disappeared into the meadow, chattering to the dog as she went.

Rachel would never see her again.

*

Once, many years before, John had asked her if she had ever seen the desert. Rachel had imagined it. She hadn't *seen* it. John knew something she didn't know.

'Once you've seen it, you'll never forget it,' he said.

It was romantic then, that thought. Now, after its heat, its aridity, its emptiness, she wanted something better.

*

Back from her ride, shaking off the sand, she switched on the TV news. It showed a snaking inferno, undulating across mountains, woods and valleys. She hoped it wasn't the place, her new place, but it was. She had longed for grass and trees, not the desert that had become a home to her. At least the desert never burned.

*

When Anja got up again before six, there was an inexplicable stillness, no bird calls, no animal sounds, a wall of grey rising behind their house, clouds drifting skywards, the forest crackling and creaking.

*

And Elvira went into her burning house, the one with the wooden awning. To save her dog.

***

Crumbs

All her life, her father tried to control her choice of partner. He became utterly infuriating when he continued to operate that control when he was dead.

'I think,' said Mike, 'I'll decorate the kitchen. A couple of coats of paint. That should do it.'

Ruth did not look up. She liked the kitchen the way it was.

'What do you think?' he said. He was examining the walls. 'Needs a good wash first,' he said. 'What's this yellowy-brown stuff on here? Looks like cigarette smoke.'

'My dad,' said Ruth.

'Oh, I get it. He was a chain smoker,' said Mike. 'You should have put your foot down and stopped that.'

Ruth said nothing.

'Need to paint this as well,' he said, swinging the door back and forward on its hinges. A cap fell off the back of the door onto the floor. 'This isn't his cap, is it?' said Mike.

'Yes,' said Ruth.

'Not that I want to criticize,' said Mike, 'but how long has he been dead?'

'Four years,' said Ruth. 'Maybe five – yes, five.'

'Well, it's about time, don't you think?' said Mike. 'I suppose that's his coat, too.'

'Yes,' said Ruth.

'Time to move on and get rid of that stuff,' said Mike.

Ruth knew in her heart of hearts that she wasn't ready to move on. Not quite. Not yet.

That's how it started, this irritation with Mike. This takeover. The planned painting of the kitchen. The advice to get rid of her dad's stuff. She wasn't having it.

It was a just a day or so later that she saw the crumbs. Mike was constantly padding about the flat, eating biscuits and miscellaneous food items rustled from the fridge and the pantry.

'Don't leave your crumbs lying around,' she told him.

'What crumbs?' he said.

Looking at the table, Ruth considered the scatter of breadcrumbs on her father's side, the side where her father sat, where her father's chair stood as it had stood all those years that he had lived in the flat.

'There,' she said and nodded towards the table.

'I never sit there,' he said. '*You* know that. It must have been you.'

She thought for a moment and then she said, 'Yes, you're right. It must have been me.' And it was her every day that followed. More breadcrumbs in the same place at the same end of the table, breadcrumbs that she swept into her hand with a silent reverence. And with the same frequency that Mike's belongings appeared randomly throughout the flat, so the crumbs appeared… as if in acknowledgement of his unwanted presence.

As she lay in bed at night, Ruth asked herself what it was that her father wanted, and did she want what her father wanted? She was, after all, her father's daughter. However much she was her own person, he was there in her blood.

Then one morning after Mike had set off for work, she put his stuff in a large box, his mug, his ties, his unread novels, his jacket, his shirt from the cleaners, his binoculars – why ever did he need binoculars? – and all the other things with which he had littered her home, so that when he returned in the evening, the box was there ready and waiting for him. What Ruth didn't want was to be cleaning up any more crumbs.

'Can't we talk about this?' said Mike. 'You're being unreasonable.'

She looked at the box. Her face softened. She looked at him. 'No,' she said.

***

Acknowledgements

Material in this collection has been previously published as follows:

'The Empty Suit' in *Sleet Magazine*; 'Holiday' in *Story Cellar*; 'Race Days' in *Strands International Lit Sphere*; 'Times Tables' in *The Arabia Review*; 'Furniture' in *Constellate Literary Journal*; 'Hotel' in *The Lakeview International Journal of Literature and the Arts*; 'Leaving' in *Strands International Lit Sphere*; 'Preparedness' in *Flash Flood*; 'Evelyn's Virtual Diary' in *Beautiful Scruffiness.*

'Gene-ius' was a *London Independent Story Prize 12th Season* finalist. 'Lost for Words' was shortlisted in the *Strand International Flash Fiction Competition*.

Sincere thanks to Robb Grindstaff for his indispensable editorial input.

A BRIEF HISTORY OF SEVERAL BOYFRIENDS

Stories

Janet Olearski

They are almost boyfriends, disgraced boyfriends, never-going-to-happen boyfriends, live-in boyfriends, dishonest boyfriends, obsessive boyfriends, dead boyfriends. Their history is brief because they didn't make the grade or, unfortunately for them, they just didn't survive.

Twenty-five thought-provoking, table-turning stories in which women stray knowingly into relationships that they may regret. And deal with them.

ISBN: 978-989-53381-4-6

A TRAVELLER'S GUIDE TO NAMISA

a novel

Janet Olearski

Philip Blair, an innocent posted abroad, must form his own judgement of Namisa, a conservative country rich in tradition, ready to embrace new beliefs on the backcloth of the Namisan *autumn-autumn* and the Pundexit Crisis. But, will having a fake marriage with Felicity, an on-the-rebound romance novelist, compromise his principles and prevent him from finding true love?

A Traveller's Guide to Namisa is an enthralling story of intercultural miscommunication, corruption, depravity, multicoloured cocktails, and PhDs.

ISBN: 978-989-53381-2-2

www.ingramcontent.com/pod-product-compliance
Lightning Source LLC
LaVergne TN
LVHW041059150826
845673LV00007B/1845

9789895338184